cellar door

An anthology of stories,
poems and essays
by University of Sydney students

SYDNEY UNIVERSITY PRESS

The University of Sydney Master of Publishing Program,
the University of Sydney
in association with the School of Letters, Art and Media
and SYDNEY UNIVERSITY PRESS
www.sup.usyd.edu.au

Quote on p. 165 is from 'Autumn' by Henry Wadsworth Longfellow (1828)
Quote on p. 167 is from 'May-Day' by Ralph Waldo Emerson (1867)
Quote on pp. 167–168 is from 'Finis' by Ella Wheeler Wilcox (1917)

Sydney University Press
Fisher Library F03
University of Sydney NSW 2006 AUSTRALIA
Email: info@sup.usyd.edu.au

National Library of Australia Cataloguing-in-Publication entry

Title:	Cellar door : an anthology of stories, poems and essays by University of Sydney students.
ISBN:	9781920899233 (pbk.)
Subjects:	Australian literature--21st century--Collections.
Other Authors/Contributors:	
	University of Sydney.
Dewey Number:	A820.8

Contents

Foreword

Writing is such a recent skill; it must be easy to understand its apparent necessity. Writers start young, when the imperatives of sex should wipe out almost everything else, but the opposite holds true. Writing, then, answers a strong urge, as if at chromosomal level our double helixes had unspooled and dropped as typeface from the box of oral history to the waiting page.

It's clear, speaking is insufficient. Having invented that, we scratched with sticks on beaches, hammered stone, furled plumes across the sky from the tail end of a plane to make written language, an art that inhabits our lonely heads, becomes our dearest neighbours, wisest friends.

Each anthology makes its own community. Here, Perveen Jeet, that plump, doleful creation of Zainab Rifaath Anver, lives next door to John Walsh's Bill and Melinda Gates; 'down the street, a clatter of life' in Siang Lu's 'A Stately Procession'; round the corner is Katie with her 'lostness' always behind her in Christopher Roche's 'Swimming'; and we agree, standing on the footpath with Rosa Campbell's Ann Aurora, that in a world 'full of unjoined things' you 'cannot ever know the velocity of the moment you are in.'

We write to make ourselves less strange, less dangerous to each other. Maria El-Chami in 'I See You Everywhere' becomes the fifteen year old Kahlil Gibran, explaining: 'You see, in Arabic, we don't pronounce the letter *p*. /imagine the words pomegranate and prayer falling like parachutes/down your knickerbocker knees.'

With this foreword, I'm glad to take part.

Rhyll McMaster

The Webs That We Weave

Amelia Walkley

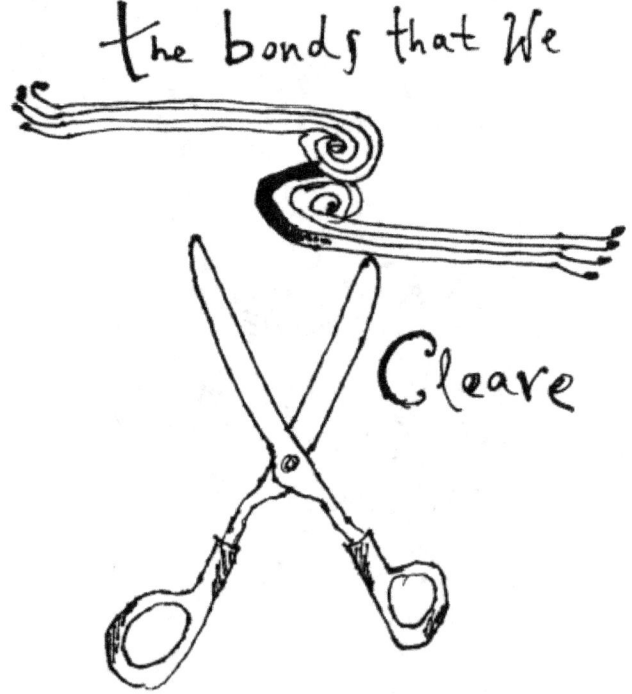

the bonds that We

Cleare

the Loves that We

Leave...

the Sighs that We
-sigh-
Heave...

Show Time

Adrian Richardson

Have you seen the show?
Its opening line is:
'*The Perfect Sphere turns effortlessly in space.*'

Reviews describe it as a mad theatrical farce, based on truth.
The setting is Time and Place and Things and Forms and
    Thoughts.
The main characters are I and You.
It has a captivating chorus of emotional soliloquies.

At the end there is an unexpected twist.
Two finales are presented.
In the first, the hero dies and curtain closes.
In the second, the curtain opens to the line:
'*The Perfect Sphere turns effortlessly in space.*'

The Adventures of Ann Aurora

Rosa Campbell

i.

From up here, in the air, Ann Aurora can see the roof where she sat for six months and watched the planes. As the sky hummed *not yet*, she, hot and sticky in her pyjamas, whisper-spoke the countdown of days:

Sixty-six; thirty; twelve.

When there was one day to go, she and he walked with a skip and a step, a hand hand heart heart. Nearly dying of restlessness as the street lights burnt and power lines cut segments into the sky around them.

Now Ann is flying, running across the tops of a thousand thousand lives; she sees the shafts of sun tethering the sky to the ground, warming the backs of the people in the suburban swimming pools below.

She wonders if some of the people doing lazy laps have lives like her own, full of boxes sealed with red tape, dust and trinkets, chocolate money, tea cups small and fine (with handles broken and un).

Ann wants to write this trip down,

all of its intricacy

breath in breath out

stowing away of the travelling tray, window watching, book reading would be recorded if it could.

ii.

This winter in Beijing, the sprawling city is covered in a cold smog mist.

Ann with thirteen million others moves along in this air that thickly snarls and tastes of pepper.

She bumps damp shoulders with strangers before she can make out their faces.

And uses the smudges of neon that penetrate the hanging grey as guiding lights.

Ann forgets there are stars in the sky.

People are around and all over, back streets fill up empty out fill up;

sweet potato sellers, people pushing rubbish up hills, three nuns in habits chatting more loudly than anyone else in the street.

Except the tourists:

Oh my god. This is the first (loud slurpy sip) *good coffee I've had since* (slurp sip *swallow* sip) *I like left Cali!* (smack lips together deep sigh of contented wealth whiteness).

(That Ann recognises, that Ann understands. That she replicates.)

Three cool girls totter around on heels like new lambs, speaking to each other and into mobile phones. Then everyone seems to leave,

the tourists donning ridiculous layers, off to photograph something

Genuinely Devastated!

And there is nothing but a gasp and a great stretch of street,

bigger than anything Ann has ever ever seen.

Maps pale in comparison.

Ann's heart beats in her chest at Tiananmen Square.

She clutches her coat sleeves hard as Chairman Mao's mausoleum stretches monstrous Stalinist architecture into the sky.

She is surrounded by farmers clutching yellow flowers to give to The Great Man.

Some weep.

Ann tries to imagine revolution without irony.

Fails.

It comes upon her often in China, the incommensurability and overwhelm of it. How, Ann wonders, can she ever do anything here, amidst the Mao and the Nike and the Coca-Cola. How can she walk! Here! How can she sit here drinking coffee! Now.

But just as soon as it seems it will never leave, the urgency of it all mattering so much and not at all seeps and ebbs out of her. Forms a pool on the linoleum floor.

She passes it squarely by, being careful not to get her feet wet as she buttons her red coat and steps out into China.

Here she goes!

In China today there is just this point, now.

Everything just at this point and right now.

Now.

And Ann realises you can never know that.

Cannot ever know the velocity of the moment you are in.

iii.

In London, under a sky that is lofty and coloured like old snow Ann finds a small, precious patch of blue in the middle of a day.

People squint like they can't believe it, tip their hats in the street towards a sun bright and strange and look up!

In this city, Ann spends a lot of time standing and admiring the light; and right now under a shining sky Ann wants to chalk out the shadows on sandstone. On the sides of buildings placed on the London street like knobs of butter, rich and solid on the side of a plate.

She would like to surprise with pink and white lines, showing the passing of time in a simple way.

She is startled by the slippage of time.

It seemed to disappear through the cracks at pristine Hong Kong Airport.

It slid into her coat pocket with two postcards of paintings that remind Ann of her self.

Hours are ticked away severely on her wrist and Ann is reminded that it is tea time.

People remember all over this city:

One thinks, in the impersonal pronoun, *that it is time for tea.*

They get out the three piece crockery, something sweet and something savoury and zig-zag together on a tray, balancing between arms and elbows.

The tea brews up strong as they wait in the centrally heated room with the Roget's Thesaurus and the board games and the Christmas tree.

Talking with frowns as they sit and sip.

And she loves it in her infatuation with the world.

But not just this, and contrary to the colour on old maps this is not all.

And she can't stay here because she could forget that

and drown in a cup of builders' tea.

It would be so *easy*.

iv.

Ann Aurora is looking out (bleary eyed) at the people carrying cheeses and trails of fairy lights.

She rubs under her eye; a man looks at her as if she might be crying. (A look made of one part apprehension and two parts empathy.)

She isn't.

But she might be finger-painting the smudge of purple shadow that sits under both her eyes and reminds her of how exhausting it is to look a lot.

For in downtown Warsaw there are:

babies wrapped up in coats,

empty sky spaces in the middle of apartment blocks,

a library with no books and no walls all stretched out for Ann to see.

In this city where things are still crumbling, the people are walking their strange human walks amongst the concrete and cinder block buildings of the sturdy sooty kind.

This morning there are bright lights and hot coffee.

And on New Year's Eve the kids let off fireworks in big amateurish sprays of pink and gold, green and purple.

It makes for an almost forgetting.

But forgetting feels furtive in this city.

Like stranger-smiles on the metro.

Ann was surprised when the first person, with more lines than face, turned up the corners of their mouth for her and just as surprised when the smile was swallowed back up into its crevice.

It, like forgetting, was unexpected and fleeting.

Warsaw is hemmed in by the gigantic and neglected Jewish cemetery. Brambles cover paths and headstones are all angles and moss covered pebbles placed there years ago by relatives visiting from America.

(Few Jews in Warsaw today.)

Ann stood there in her boots and her stockings trying to comprehend.

Wondering about Palestine and reasoning and righteousness.

Trying to see through the blur.

Wondering where it is that she fitted into all of this.

And not wanting this tragedy to become her she wondered what was really being felt under the weight bearing down on her body.

And today she wants to sit and talk about watching the school boys with their willowy arms and the woman juggling her briefcase stepping in the pools of pavement light.

She is full of enormous yawns and thoughts on this first day of January two-thousand-and-seven.

But she doesn't speak or move or laugh or breathe or write.

She feels that it's the least she can do.

This entire city is a memorial.

v.

Ann in Alexanderplatz talks vaguely to a Polish boy about home.
(doesn't miss it, doesn't talk like some of the others who craft
Australian sunsets and best-beaches-in-the-world out of raucous
laughs and dancing hands)

Mostly though they just sit smoking rolled up cigarettes, the
sour tobacco burning brightly down to their knuckles.

He points to the glowing orange, asks her

Is this how hot Australia is?

Ann laughs, blowing smoke into the day and thinks as it tendrils
upwards:

Things happen here.

The things, the happenings, seem to echo, bouncing and moving
in Berlin.

And it feels all a little

Haven't we already? (as the typewriters tic tic ding)

Haven't we before sometime? (as the cameras clic whir)

This city has seen it all.

Bohemia, empire, fall, wall, crumble.

And now.

On Tuesday Ann goes dancing in an old Stasi lounge emerging
with another into the cold dark. They walk, past squats and doors
more street art than door.

They order coffee and share it warming their hands on it and
each other as they pass a bouquet of flowers outside the Jewish
Museum. The flowers look blacker than the night.

(six million, six million, Ann thinks)

As the sun tints the black sky grey, they run their hands along the kilometre stretch of wall still standing. They listen on the bridge as the river Spree slaps its banks below.

Ann listens to the tap shoes, tin cans, opera, sound of paint-brushes, din of thinking. She hears the new art reverberate off the old and wonders why you would ever add to the noise.

But then the sky is the colour of slate and cracked through with light.

It hangs effortlessly over Berlin,

a silent beauty

not yet full.

vi.

Ann Aurora is flying back to the city famous for its harbour, famous for its seas.

She has three pieces of the Berlin wall in her pocket and some ironic tourist t-shirts for friends and non-ironic tourist t-shirts for grandparents

And a vague sense of being hollowed out.

On day one-hundred-and-thirteen when she packed her bag for the last time, she left a story in a pile under her pillow.

She had bound it tightly in twine and packed it when she began:

Ann had expected to come home and say after her one hundred plus days in her almost transatlantic accent;

It was exactly like I expected it to be.

But she can't, because it wasn't.

Ann had expected to find a piece of sky cut out for her, exactly.

And she did for short bursts, quick shocks.

As if the people were waiting for her to arrive with her red coat and her dirty blue backpack, shaking out the night from her hair, before they began to talk and drink their coffee.

But for the most part it was not this way.

There is much too much, much too much too much too much for a shuddering together of world and self.

A fulfilling of mythologies and a filling of heart.

The world is full of unjoined things.

This is how it is today, with the great staggering expanse of blue surrounding her.

Marine Parade

Matthew Fenwick

I go down to Mahon Pool for a night swim. When the tide's up, the handrails are almost underwater, and the surge washes right across the rock platform and into the rock pool there. Waves explode on the seawall and spill foam over it. This is the best time. The pool's got swell, but it's contained by the four walls. It's tricky where the steps meet the water, all slick with this green velvet algae. You plant your feet and they're refracted, like under brown bottle-glass. You're still land-bound, though, and the surge can drag you to the rocks and crack your skull. You grip the rails, then launch yourself on the next surge, flopping like some crazy-brained flying machine.

Then you just float and let the waves do the moving for you.

I don't come in the daytime. The place is full of ear-piercing little shitheads and their dogs. Old men lapping and heaving their saggy tits and pot-stove bellies out of the water, dripping. Speedos, for God's sake.

I'm not much into open surf either. This ocean goes all the way to Peru and none of it's anyone's. The breakers roll right over you, then draw you back out, stuffing you with sand in the process.

Down at the rock pool it's usually pretty dark and private. Lovers straddle on the headlands and do their thing with the moon. Rock fishermen inch crablike round the point with buckets and rods. But we leave each other alone, so it's fine.

Tonight, there's someone there. I see them soon as I got out of my car, and I say a little fuck to myself. A couple, yellow in the flood-lights. Skinny-dipping teenagers, probably. Christ, there goes my evening. I guess I feel a bit less sour seeing I've spoiled their romantic evening too. Getting closer now, I see one of them's no teenager. He's silver-haired and black-shirted. Stocky. That old-man type who want you to know they can still bench press and pull a root. Something German about his face.

She's got tangled black hair and a slick singlet. Skinny, though. Too skinny for me. Legs straight down. She turns and under her ribs is hollowed out.

I make my footfalls heavy so they'll register I'm here and not start getting all porno on me. Gunter draws back from his girlfriend. He looks up at me, eyes in shadow. I could be a council inspector — I'm sorry, sir, nakedness is not permitted.

Sky pushes a towel at him, gives me a quick look-over and goes on ahead.

'Hi,' he says. He's got these ice-clear eyes.

'Hi.'

'So you think you go for a swim?' The accent fits my Euro-perve suspicions.

'Sure.'

'It's dangerous?'

'Nah, it's fine if you know what you're doing.'

Sky strides barefoot along the wall of the rock pool. A low chain loops between stakes driven into the rock. Gunter fingers this gold cross at his neck and watches her go.

'So are you going in?' I ask.

'No. The water is too dark for me.' Probably where he's from there's just sludgy rivers with fuming chemical plants on the sides.

'I just watch you both.'

Okay. Enjoy. Take pictures.

I undress in a shadow away from him. Pull off my trousers. Stash my wallet in the toe of my work shoes and stuff a sock in after it. Hide them under my trousers. I pick my way down to the steps where the sea swills over my feet. Tonight, there's a slick of moonlight running from me right out to the horizon, and the moon's low in the sky. The light's so solid you could almost walk right out along it.

This water's perfect. The mistake everybody makes is that the sea's going to be icy cold, but it's not. Even when the air goes wintery, there's still enough summer in the water to swim. The cold just nips at your ears.

In here's as safe as I get, in this ocean box. The waves carry me about, but nothing's taking me out to sea. I do breaststroke, only my eyes above water, and I watch the wavelets on waves. They're always turning into something else.

Sky is having a Titanic moment on the seawall, hair streaming back. Waves break around her. She just grips the chain through the whitewash and throws her head back. She's shouting something out to sea.

This is all wrong. Gunter should be on the ramparts, barrel-chested and braving the waves, and she should be back there at the cave mouth, sending beams of admiration at him. But he stays by the rock ledge, holding her towel to himself. He looks scared of her.

I feel useless, bobbing around in my box with them doing their dumb slow show for me.

Personally, I don't mind women who are a little bit nuts sometimes. If it was me, I'd go round to her, and pull her off the chain, and we'd fall in together and go under. The camera would go underwater with us and you'd just see blue-black water and a plume of white bubbles.

I've never been up there, on the breakwater in high surf. I don't know why — it's just one of those things that I've never done. Like smoking pot, going on a road trip, missing a whole night's sleep, going bungee jumping. I never got round to it.

I haul myself out, and my board shorts cling to my things. Wet, wrinkled and dark. I'm thinking of her legs again. I shake the water off.

Gunter steps forward to me.

'Ah hello!' he says warmly, like we actually know each other. He's got that fake red-cheeked friendliness of Germans on beer posters.

'Hi.'

Sky is still over there, facing seaward, facing off the waves.

'Was it good?' he asks.

'It's nice, but probably nicer round at Coogee rock pool. Very romantic. You should go there next time. It's better for you.'

'Romantic? What is this?'

'Oh, romantic is when two people...'

'Yes, my English is okay thanks. In your country twenty years I have been.'

Is he taking the piss? I didn't think Germans did sarcasm.

'Oh,' he says. 'You think Kara is my lover?'

I look around for my shoes.

He chuckles coldly. 'Australians. You jump to conclusion like that.' He snaps his fingers. 'Kara is my stepdaughter. I bring her down here sometimes and maybe the water makes her calm for a while.'

'Oh, okay. That's cool.'

'Not exactly cool. My daughter is sick. This crazy ice she takes. It makes her strong. And she has no fear.' He wipes a hand down his face, over his eyes. 'But me, I look at the sea, and I look at her and I have fear.'

This is one of those times when you're in black water, and you don't know if the bottom's ten centimetres below your toes or you're 50 metres out of your depth.

Over by the railing, there's no girl. Waves breaking over where she'd stood. I check the man. Should I tell him? He's gazing back behind us to where the lights arc around Marine Parade.

'Everybody does things when they're young. Smoke pot and get maybe a bit crazy. You know?'

'Sure,' I say.

'But she just keeps taking it, and I keep... getting angry. Sometimes I kick her out and tell her to take the druggy shit and go. But then I worry. This way is better.'

19

'Will she be okay?' This is what you say, isn't it? I feel like I'm reciting a script I haven't practised enough.

He looks at me sharply, then down. 'Either she will be okay, or... she will not be okay.'

'That sounds hard.'

'I can do nothing. I just hope my stepdaughter stays on the right side of the chain.'

'Reeeeooooarrr!'

She lands on all fours on the boulder table and there's water dripping from hems and crotch. Hair down around the face. I only see a flash of her eyes, primitive and dilated.

Then she stands. Wraps herself round her dad. Presses her sopping, sheeny body to him. He sighs. Pulls the white towel around them both and the two of them are enclosed.

Tonight I don't go straight home. Shower. TV. Bed. I drive past that Italian place off Marine Parade. It's that type of Italian joint with plastic tablecloths and candles in bottles with centuries of wax, the kind of place the headland lovers call 'our place.' I get strawberry gelato in a cone, clean the taste of salt away. I sit out on the bench with the sweethearts going dovey inside, sharing pizza. Out at sea, there's the luminous grey mass of the breakers. I think about Sky standing in the middle of them, daring them to take her out.

On the other side of the street there's a stack of apartments. I watch all these people in there, separate and swimming around in their little boxes with their TVs flickering at the windows.

I See You Everywhere

Maria El-Chami

*The Lebanese poet and artist Kahlil Gibran moved to America
in 1895. Three years later, he was introduced to the charismatic
Josephine Preston Peabody at a photographic exhibition at the
Boston Camera Club. He was fifteen years old.*

In the centre of the Camera Club, Josephine twirls
a curl and recites her poetry. All I have is an apology
for calling her *Miss Beabody*.

My english —
crooked A B Cs
she does not laugh, though I still feel foolish
frowning at the vision of myself
a few whiskers, my long black hair
like David without a slingshot.

You see, in Arabic, we don't pronounce the letter *p*.
imagine the words pomegranate and prayer falling like
    parachutes
down your knickerbocker knees.

I try to keep quiet but my fez is full of questions.
For instance, what would it be like to match a moustache in a
    portrait?
To orbit the room with an opinion on the stars and the moon,
to borrow from Blake without stumbling over commas and full
    stops.

Men in tuxedoes pull out their cameras
to teach Josephine how to catch a close up.
Her eyes squint, her hand twirls, my velvet suit flashes red.

She walks over to me and says, *I see you everywhere, look —*
on the wall, various poses: me wearing a khafiya, holding
    a sword,
fingering sentences in an open book.
But you look so sad, she adds.

Miss Peabody, I say.
I repeat it until it sounds straight,
until it makes her blush and turn away.

Exhale

Raymond Baltas

I breathe in
and exhale words that
both break and
mend your feet
I tell you I can't sleep anymore
and you ask me why
but I don't know
I'm playing with hair
that's not really yours
because it's not really hair
I'm sitting back cushioned
in the front seat
of your hatchback
even though I'm actually
outside in a chilled paddock
where my breath draws
ghost trails
and the stars are
shining as if for the
last time
I tell you that some where
out there

beyond the display window
of the world,
I loved you, and I love you.
I'm exhaling words
that lull your head
into the deepest of
sleeps, but I myself still can't sleep
although I'll pretend,
just for you,
just for us,
just for this one precious
night as we lay on
the prickly green blades
in your little red hatchback.

I wake up in bed, it's almost 4 am,
and all I remember saying is goodnight.

Fiend

Nicole Chunge

Malicious sleuth lurking amongst the interior

By creeping, yet unhurried, ready to pounce

The heart is unaware, naive and raw

Seduced and encompassed by the dark

The fall is foreboden by the all-knowing mind

And the heart is hit

Slowly, slowly

The flourish of innocence now

Fading, fading

A reminder to the soul that the world is not for trusting

Chicken

Colin Dray

Steve was dead. Not *dead* dead, but dead asleep. He looked dead on the outside, but on the inside I could tell he was dreaming. About surfing maybe, or playing the pokies. Or me. He's the only person I know who laughs in his sleep. All the time. He'll kick his feet — that's what usually wakes me up, his toenails on my leg — and his whole body wriggles as he lets out a soft, slow chuckle. It's like when kids laugh; as though they're showing you the feeling it gives them under their skin. But Steve didn't realise. He was asleep the whole time, wriggling out his little joke. And this time he was dead to it.

I had been up since five. Vomiting, washing my face. But the noise didn't wake him. Not me. Not the toilet flushing. Not when I left for the all-night chemist. When I came back he was still there, sprawled across the mattress, one elbow twisted in the bed sheets. I closed the door so I wouldn't bother him. I peed on the stick. Waited twenty minutes. Sat biting my hand on the edge of the bath, smiling.

At nine, when he still hadn't moved, I tried to get him up. At first I tapped him on the arm, whispered, 'Come on, Steve,' in the voice I use when babysitting the girls across the street. But he just lay there. I tried putting the kettle on and rattling the dishes in the kitchen. I nudged him. I tapped his cheek. But when his chest finally lifted he just burped the stale scent of beer into my face.

'You'll be late,' I said. 'They'll fire you.'

He hiccuped, and I heard something coming up in his throat.

I reminded him he'd been late the past three weeks. Told him his boss was leaving angry messages.

He groaned and rolled on his side.

His suit was crumpled in a heap at the bottom of the wardrobe. I tugged it out and laid it flat on the bed so it would straighten. There was a damp stain on the left shoulder. It was sticky, and smelt sweet, like bourbon. He must have worn it the night before. He did that sometimes. He thinks it's funny.

I shook him again gently. Petted his chest. Rubbed the tip of my nose on his forehead. But he was dead to it all.

The phone rang, and I knew it would be Steve's boss. I let it ring through to the machine. 'Steven?' I heard his boss say. The voice cleared its throat and left a moment's silence. The line crackled. 'Steven, now this is too much.'

I looked down at the bed, at the suit and the tangle of blankets. Steve was almost smiling. I made a decision. I folded the suit up in my arms and walked out the door.

Steve has his own parking space at the side of the stadium. Sometimes, when we come early, Steve lets me wait in the car with the radio running until his father arrives. I pulled up and turned off the car. I climbed over into the back seat where the suit was laid out, drying. Fans wandered past in guernseys and face paint, drinking. Nobody seemed to notice me. I sank as far out of sight as I could and started to pull Steve's pants on over my jeans. His shoes were loose, and hung heavy on my ankles. The gloves were hot on my palms. As I tugged the top over my chest, the sweat in the fabric felt cold against my skin. When I set the head of the suit on my shoulders I choked a little on Steve's odour. His underarms and the chocolaty smell of his tobacco. I stretched up to look in the rear vision mirror. Stiff plastic eyes stared back. I was the team mascot. I was a chicken.

People started noticing me on the way into the stadium. They called out, pointed and shouted, and when I gave a little wave they laughed. The security guards let me through to the locker rooms, nodding hello.

'Steve,' they said. I smiled beneath the head.

'All right,' the team manager said when he saw me drop Steve's backpack beside his locker. 'I thought you were going to leave us wanting.' He came over to pat my shoulder, his hand squeezing the material of the suit. I wondered quickly if he could tell my arm was thinner.

Through the doorway of the bathroom two of the team's players were standing naked beneath the showers. The closest was a forward I usually liked to watch when I'm sitting in the crowd. On the field he seems bronzed and walks with a bit of a swagger. He skips, his legs slicing the air as he sprints across the field, the ball pressed to his chest. But here, he and the other player looked shorter than I remembered. Smaller. Suddenly I felt uncomfortable seeing them exposed. Almost queasy again. The water hissed horribly on their bare skin. Amongst the steam and the yellow tiles they looked old and leathery.

The manager was telling me to forget about the messages he'd left. 'Heat of the moment, and all that,' he said. 'Just make sure you're here from now on.' He said something about value, about the role being mine. His. Steve's.

Something shoved me from behind, and when I turned, one of the team subs — Damien — was pushing past. He nodded to the manager while unzipping his bag, and then to me. To Steve.

I remembered Damien from a team party Steve had taken me to once. The players, the members and families — all out at some beach house on the coast. Steve had been gone most of the night, playing cricket and smoking out on the sandbanks, and when I lost my jacket it was Damien who found it under a couch cushion.

'So Steve,' Damien was saying. 'Where's your girlfriend?' His smile was odd, from one side of his mouth. It made his face seem thinner and pale. 'She wasn't out in the car.'

I stiffened for a moment. I wondered if he'd seen me getting changed. But he didn't appear to be testing me. He just looked angry.

I shrugged, stepping out of view of the showers. The two players inside had started laughing at something, their stomachs jerking awkwardly, their flesh in a spasm. It made me feel dirty to watch. Even the sound, echoing, made me uncomfortable.

The manager slapped me again. 'Fifteen minutes!' he announced to the room and wandered away.

Damien kept staring, unbuttoning his shirt and kicking his shoes under the bench. 'She up in the stands already?' He was slipping his guernsey on. 'Or is she not here today?'

Not sure what to do, I just stood there, the suit feeling heavier on my neck.

'She at home?' he said, and this time his lips were tight. 'Is she sick?' He seemed to be looking straight in at me, through the black gauze over my face. He was squinting. Glaring. His fingers were clutching his belt. I smelt a tang of bourbon from inside the suit. I opened my mouth to explain.

'She's a good chick,' he said. He hissed through his nose, bending over to change his pants. 'She doesn't — '

He stopped, shaking his head. He slid his shorts up his legs and slapped the bag shut.

'Just don't be a fucking prick,' he said, and slumped back onto the bench, holding his socks. Before he rolled them on I watched him pick the lint from between his toes.

Behind him, players were scratching themselves. Clearing their throats, coughing into the sink with a wet slap. Someone was peeing with the toilet stall open and I saw him shudder his legs when he flushed and retied his shorts. I'd never seen anyone do that before; like the way a horse shakes flies from its skin. More showers were hissing in the next room. A guilty, hollow feeling crept over me again. I swallowed down the taste in my mouth.

When I stepped out into the stadium, sunlight lit up the cracks in the suit. White outlines warmed the edges of its eyes and along the neck. There was music playing into the stands, soft and metallic over the speakers, and I could see the crowd above settling into place.

Laughter. People rubbing sunscreen into their skin. Eskies shuffling across laps. Waving signs.

Up by the edge of the concession stand, Steve's father was sitting alone beside an empty seat. My seat. His face was scrunched up, and he was squinting even though the sun wasn't in his eyes. He had one elbow hooked over the back of my seat, and he wasn't chatting to the people around him like we do when I'm there. He just sat slumped in place, looking past me down at the field. When I waved at him he nodded back. His face didn't change. He thought I was Steve. I felt a slight chill.

The manager tapped me with his clipboard. 'Wakey, wakey,' he said. 'Better get started.'

He gestured to somewhere behind me, out of sight, and a moment later the team anthem started up on a small stereo. At first the sound was swallowed by the crowd but slowly people began to take notice. Some turned to look. Some sang along to the lyrics. Children sat forward in their seats. Steve's father crossed his arms. I stood facing them. The suit felt lopsided across my chest. Everyone was waiting.

In the shadows of the dressing room corridor the cheerleaders were waving at me to start. Whoever was running the music stopped the song and started it again. There was a groan.

'Dance, chicken,' someone called.

People laughed. There was rustling and coughing and chatter. I thought I was going to vomit. My skin prickled. My forehead was wet. My legs and arms were aching and felt like lead. Every ripple of the crowd pounded against my head. But I'd seen Steve do the moves to his dance every week. I'd seen him practice them at home when he's drinking. I balled my hands into fists. I felt the sweat on my palms.

I kicked my leg out. There was a shout. I bobbed a little. I started to shuffle and hop and sway. People began clapping. The loose material of the suit slapped against my skin and the scent of mildew and liquor churned around my head. The claps in the stand started to come together. I stepped up onto the bench. The boots thumped with every step. Eventually I couldn't hear the music properly through the costume, but the crowd had a rhythm so I danced along. At first I just wiggled a little, but soon I was leaping. Swinging my arms. I danced with a football. I shook my bottom. I ran in circles. Suddenly there were cheerleaders around me. Pressing against me. Legs and arms and dresses. Pom-poms. Colour. Cheers. I was free behind the suit. I was gone. Not sick. Not hot. Not me. I was the chicken. Dancing. I was Steve. His clothes. His job. His smell. I shimmied like him. I gave high fives. I ran over and kicked the other team's mascot in the udders. It was a cow. I was a chicken. I was free. When we stopped, the players came out and the stadium roared so loud I felt the suit tremble. It was like I was in something alive.

The cheerleaders were circling me, panting. I remembered how bright they had always seemed from the stands. How shiny. But close up their costumes were faded and matted with dirt. Their pom-poms were strips of thick plastic that left red marks on their fingers and each of the girls had grass stains under their knees. As the noise died down I realised one of them was whispering in my ear. Her voice was close and quiet. It went up and down. Almost musical. Saying something about being excited.

' — too late last night,' I heard her say as she led me back to the bench. 'I thought I'd worn you out.' Her hand tugged on my wrist. The suit's wrist. Steve's wrist. She lifted both our hands, pressing them into her hip, turning to curl our arms around her waist.

'What did you tell her when you got home?' She was smiling, dusting off the back of her dress. Arching her spine. 'Is that why she's not here? Is she gone?'

I said my name. It sounded distant as it was muffled by the suit.

'I guess you'll be all alone after the game?' she said. 'No one to help you get out of that?'

She was smiling into my face. The chicken's face.

'Do you want some help?' She squinted and smiled.

I must have slouched. The suit's head tipped forward, jerking my neck. The window through the chicken's mouth pointed at her chest. She laughed. 'Good,' she said. She kept staring in at me, trying to make out Steve's eyes amongst the shadow. Her skin was dry and leathery. She wasn't even pretty.

A siren blew. The cheerleaders spread apart again, whooping and leaping. Flashes of colour. I stood in place. The bench against my leg. The suit felt clammy, and as she ran past with the others she slapped my tail. The thump echoed around the material. I watched her run onto the field, hazy through the black mesh. There was more roaring, but it sounded further way.

The rest of the day was a blur. The moments smeared together. There was clapping. Whistles. Music, dull and thumping. The girl came back to rustle her pom-poms in my face. They made a slithering sound. The crowd swirled, a mass of arms and mouths and shouts. It surged and rumbled and hissed. Face paint and skin. Steve's father was lost in the noise. I wanted to throw up but my stomach, all of me, felt empty. I left before the final goal was kicked.

When I got home Steven was still asleep, still curled in bed snoring. I undressed quietly, folded up the suit and placed it by the window. I sat beside it, rubbing the patch of bourbon, still sticky, between my fingers. The sun was hot on the other side of the blinds, its glow seeping into the room, red and buttery. I could still see the test and its box where I'd left them on the bathroom sink. On the other side of the room, half out of the covers, Steve's bare chest and face seemed to shine. His odour was still in my hair. His sweat still chilling my skin. The same little kid smile still playing on his lips. He was probably dreaming. Something inside him tickling, wriggling to get out.

Five Blocks

Katia Audencial

It was 1.30 in the morning and one of the coldest nights I had experienced in Sydney so far. After a long night, everyone was either drunk, lazy, tired or asleep. So when Brian asked who wanted to get a bite to eat, I was the only one who responded in the affirmative. One of the few who bothered to respond actually.

Barely twenty seconds had passed since my feet landed on the footpath and already I felt as if a bucket of ice-cold water had been poured all over my body. I stuffed my hands into my coat pockets and wondered if I would ever get used to winter, to all this cold. The necessity of having to wear several layers of clothes, even when staying indoors, was such a foreign concept to me. I had spent the last twenty years of my life knowing only two seasons: wet and dry. I missed the humidity and heat of Manila. Even the months when one typhoon after another would waltz in and out of the country did not seem half as bad compared to this. There was endless rain for days, but at least it was never this cold.

Brian warned me that the only place he knew that was still open at this hour was four or five blocks away.

'What the heck,' I said. 'I'm really hungry. We might as well give it a shot.' We started walking.

Several minutes passed by in silence before Brian asked, 'You're an English major right?'

'Yes,' I said, smiling. I was surprised that he remembered as we had only talked once, when a mutual friend introduced us to one another. But then I also remembered several things about him from that conversation — economics major, grew up in Brisbane, living in a dorm on campus, liked to surf and play basketball.

By the time we bought our chicken kebabs and sat down at one of the tables we had pretty much fulfilled the getting-to-know-you stage. We had gone the whole favourite movie/bands/TV shows/book, number of siblings, parents' jobs, places we grew up and plans after graduation route.

Then he asked, 'Why did your family move to Australia?'

This was a question that had been thrown at me dozens of times before, so I found myself repeating a response I had given in previous conversations which seemed to satisfy other people's curiosity. 'My parents wanted to move here because they thought it would be a better place for us to live in. Stable economy, great health care and wonderful landscapes. Also, more opportunities for my brothers and I in terms of establishing ourselves financially and furthering our careers. In the Philippines, succeeding often has a lot more to do with who you know, where you studied and your social background, than anything else. Unless you're insanely smart or incredibly lucky.'

He nodded. 'Do you miss living in the Philippines?'

'Yes. Terribly. I wish we never had to leave but I love my parents for making the decision. I can't say that I love being here, at least not yet, but I'm grateful that I am.' I paused. 'It isn't home. I'm not sure it ever will be. In the meantime I guess I'm just waiting for someone or something to make it all worthwhile.'

'Well, I hope you do find that something. Or someone.' He smiled.

'Thanks.'

There was a lull.

'So, I'm stuffed. I don't think I can finish this anymore. You want it?' I asked, handing him my half-finished kebab. He laughed then took it from my hands.

***

Four stores down, I sat on a bench beside Brian. He wanted to smoke.

'Do you mind?' He asked.

'No of course not,' I replied, although sometimes I did.

He asked me if I had a boyfriend. I told him I'd never had one. He seemed surprised like most people. I'm used to it. But unlike others, he left it at that. For once I didn't feel like I had to defend myself, as if it were such a crime.

I threw the question back at him. He was silent for a moment before confessing that there was an ex-girlfriend who broke up with him a year ago.

'She wasn't up for a long-distance relationship. Her dad was transferred to London and they were all going to move there.'

He told me how they first met and had slowly progressed from being friends to more than that. I found out that he was the romantic type of boyfriend, a gentleman too.

'We were together for two years and I loved her so much.'

I couldn't help it; I placed my hand on his arm and lightly squeezed.

'She just didn't love me that much, I guess.'

'I'm sorry. You're a great guy, I hope you didn't have to go through too much.'

He didn't say anything for a while. He just smiled weakly back at me and then flicked his cigarette to the ground before stepping on it with his foot.

'We should probably go,' he said. I stood up.

We started walking back. In the cold Sydney air, we passed the same empty, barely-lit streets. We talked of home, of the things we'd done and were willing to do for our families, of the relationships we had formed here. We talked of people and moments that had broken our hearts, and of dreams we had realised that were never meant for us. But despite it all, still being able to find that faint glimmer of hope to hold on to. I couldn't remember the last time I had talked with someone so openly or candidly. Or remember being out that late on strange streets, with a boy I barely knew, feeling so completely at peace.

For the first time since I arrived in this foreign land, I was certain I was where I needed to be.

Five blocks later we were back where we came from. I lingered outside with him for as long as I could, wishing that there were another twenty blocks ahead of us.

Paths

Amelia Walkley

I

Particle-like
ebb and float
ocean-swallowed
and flailing,
suspended in the salt and the sea
finding me
and counting
that horizon line
stretched forever
timeless, in its eternities
though mere seconds passed
sun sparked and joyous
I lay like Jezebel in the water.

II

Tempted, like an Eve
I conjure stars
and think of loves, ready-made
forged with bellows
fanning fires long wasted and spent
barefoot in my haste,

and before it is too late,
I am running to the smithy
lest this crack force itself deeper
lest my iron heart remain
a jagged collection of puzzle pieces
that nobody can solve
because some of them are missing.

III

Here I stride
into the womb of Tamar's night
glide, glide the twisting road
I am swallowed by cascading light
and I find solace
in this, my plight
the evening shades, hesitates.
The golden frowning moon
and pins of star
scar
the bruised and tempered sky
my footsteps print the road,
and mark my life.

Moon

Ruth Stubbings

The moon died tonight.
She melted and bled and drowned the Earth
with her purple milk and frightened stars,
forcing you upon your roof to gaze
at a black dead sky
and dangle your legs over the moonriver
where the stars tattoo themselves to your worn feet.
Now there is a reason to worship the ground you walk on...

A Stately Procession

Siang Lu

Sunlight through the slats. Gentle stirring in bed. The saturation of consciousness whisking away the dregs of sleep. Lie awake and listen to the muffled sounds of an indifferent city. Strangled traffic, mewling neighbours, some kind of birdsong.

Bedcovers thrown off, shed like a skin.

New day new experience. But I've done this before.

Yes, all my life.

Get up with practiced ease. Feet kicking away at stray clothes and scattered books and all manner of bedroom detritus. Find the floor, test for solid ground to be stood on. You can never be sure. Successful navigation to the bathroom. Confused state of waking life. Something to be acted out in familiar beats and measures. A yawn. I need a shave.

Look at that idiot, brushing his teeth in the mirror. Who does he think he's fooling?

Remember to throw out the milk, remember her birthday. How old is she now? Two years younger than Leanne, who is a year younger than me. That's — what — nineteen? Nineteen. Remember the rent, remember the chiropractor, what else?

Brush, brush, brush.

Remember to spit, of course.

A Colgate swirl of saliva and blood. This is nothing new. If it's a daily occurrence, it doesn't alarm you anymore.

***

'Circular motions,' I am saying, 'like they taught in grade school.'

'*Teach...*' says Clare. She is correcting me.

'It's all I can think about, brushing my teeth in circular motions.'

'... It's *teach* and not *taught*, you know...'

'What I mean is, what if things have changed?' I ask.

'... Because they don't ever stop *teaching* it, not really...'

'What if the circular brushing motion has been scientifically disproven?' I pause to sneeze.

'That's very solipsistic of you, bless you, to think of it as *taught*. Teachers are still teaching it, you know. It's not like they stopped after teaching you and called it a day.'

'What if circular motions have been undermined, overturned? Maybe the world is brushing in triangular motions.'

'Dodecahedral,' she suggests.

'Yes. And no one has yet had the common decency to tell me?' A change in the life curriculum, unbeknownst to us.

'Are you okay?' she asks, finally.

'I miss you.'

Unbearable pause, and then her soft voice, 'I don't think you should call anymore.'

I am thinking of a joke, appropriate, inappropriate, anything will do.

'You need to get out there,' she says, 'do something.'

The phone grows hot in my hand.

'Meet someone new,' she tries again.

Hang up silently. Listen to the fading static. It's the only way.

***

All this background noise.

Walk slowly to the door. Avoid the wet laundry hanging about the apartment in all sorts of ridiculous corners. From every possible precipice. The table ledge, the fridge door. Soapy water collecting on my floor in puddles of conspiracy. Step outside. Emerge into a spare, uncertain world. Proof of existence is measured in decibels. Audible grunt as I pull on sneakers. Gentle slamming of front door, feet against the blistering pavement. Sound for the sake of sound...

Inspect the clouds. Hope it doesn't rain. These are the only dry clothes I have left, found in the back of the closet and thrown on in a fit of desperation. Old chinos. Baggy t-shirt. An outfit from — what — two years ago? I have regressed, I think to myself as the familiar slouch returns, the hands shoved in pockets. I feel as if I am wearing a past-self.

I cross paths with a neighbour. Dilemma: to make eye contact or not? It doesn't matter. She initiates. 'Good morning,' she ventures kindly. The old woman a set of wrinkles and greys and interchangeable mothball sweaters. I've seen her around, this woman who wishes me 'good morning' when we pass on the street. Or else some variation of it, like 'good afternoon', like 'good evening'. As if the goodness of a thing were established fact merely for her having said it, as opposed to some shaky proposition of which one cannot be entirely sure except in retrospect.

I wave back and say 'hello' and 'yes, I hope so'.

Down the street, a clatter of life.

Look out bus windows, fiddle with pocket change.

How long would it take to know a new city, completely and intimately? Darlinghurst, Surry Hills, Cleveland Street... Disembark into this microscopic life, with its networks of curved lane and intersecting street like lines on my palm. Explore endlessly. This is how it should be with places, with people.

New day: new route. Otherwise resign yourself to tread the same familiar paths, and curse yourself for doing so.

Left, right, left, hmm, then left. Go. Exorcise all doubt. Move through this world without fear. Do not betray outward uncertainties. Walk along designated paths with familiar gait, relaxed.

Quaint suburb. A boutique store here, second-hand bookshop there, and sprouting from the side streets, the bakeries and florists a person might pass by and identify by smell alone. A good place to set the scenes of future heartbreaks.

Look up at the clouds cracking open with their cheerful promises of rain.

***

Here by the quiet cafe window.

There is a girl sitting in the corner, reading the paper. I watch her silently, through the angled reflection of my window, so she will not know my thoughts.

An over-chewed piece of gum rolls around my mouth.

Her slender hands, the faded parka she wears so comfortably, that sleepy sigh.

It would not be entirely true to say that I am in love with her, though she is indeed lovely, with the paper in her hands and her eyes forming concerned shapes as she receives the sombre news of the world.

The thing is, I never know when is the correct time to spit out my gum, that's the thing. The only thing I know is I am the type to go on and on, chewing that tasteless piece of cud, and only becoming aware of it long after the fact.

She has a boyfriend, of course. Here he is, bearing gifts of caffeine and kisses and low murmurs in ears. I have seen them, this couple, from time to time. On my first day, for example, and then on Thursday. And now, overhearing snatches of conversation.

Like, 'Really?' and 'Yes, I think so too. Tonight, then?'

Like, 'Yes, she practised a year to get it that low, and did you know Bogie fell in love with her voice in the end? So she had to keep playing it the rest of her life. Imagine that.'

These are the things he says. He could be me. I could be him. Easily. Or not easily, I guess. But why not?

They leave.

I go to their table to take the paper they have left behind. Walk past the bin. Remember to spit, of course. Spit out the gum between your teeth, but not the teeth between your gums. It's harder than it looks.

I sit back down and flip through the pages, mindlessly. World news, business, crossword, the comics next to the obituaries, everything in ordered lines of black and white... Look at my blackened hands, fingersmudged with ink. This is what I can't stand, the way things are forever rubbing off on me.

My pocket buzzes. I reach for the phone and put it to my ear. Say 'hello', watch the rain outside, with droplets racing down these weeping windows. It is my mother, whose voice cracks as she says 'hi', and I hang up, knowing it is time for me to go home.

***

Here we are, gathered at the dining table and trotting out these familiar masks of grief. And I, the only son, have been seated by the women of this family at the head of the table. A chair of antique design with high curling armrests so I cannot pull it close to the table, with a deep and recessed back so I cannot slouch, as is my usual custom.

My father used to fill this seat, whenever we would come to visit. Now it's mine. Ascension and birthright: the only way to progress in this world is to kill your fathers, your forefathers, all who came before you. If not, then deny, run breathlessly away. Flee. From the cold bedpan, the unsympathetic clipboard. From the wasted man you once knew. Well. Anything but that.

Dinner is served. Inspect it closely, this casserole from the cretaceous. Poke it with a dull utensil. This is, I imagine, how autopsies are carried out. It can't be too different. I stick it in my mouth, taste it cautiously.

My grandmother at the other end of the table, head slumped and motionless. Deathly motionless, and I am thinking oh God, she is dead too, sitting here at this sad table. And I am about to cry out in alarm until I realise she is only saying Grace to herself.

Then she opens her eyes, looking up, lively, and it is time to eat.

I look to my mother, her tear-streaked face, the coffee stains in the tiniest corners of her mouth, and she smiles to me, this tiny, imperceptible smile. And somehow it is only now that I know, stupidly, that everyone I love and cherish will be taken from me, pulled straight from the heart and into some nether world into which I may not go.

Chew this grief away.

They pass around a photo album. I run my hands along its spine and dusty remnants. Open it up, this catalogue of memory in black-and-white, where the mind may wander and guess at the brightness of day and burst colour that held such past lives.

There is the family, etched in history. My grandparents at the base of a knotted oak tree, standing comically far apart. Their son, my father. A child, peeking mischievously from the boughs above.

Another page, another era. My father's life flashing in front of my eyes. Flip, flip, flip, and now he is the familiar old man I knew. With that eternally serious face — looking more and more like his own father. Look at the still photos — their faces, whose nature and countenance seem somehow to change in death as if these strips of celluloid were themselves aware of mortal fates. My father, the severe-looking man, peering out from plastic sleeves. And I know that I will be a severe-looking man one day. It's not such a bad thing to know, I guess.

A glance at my watch. I can still catch Clare's thing if I hurry. Sneak in through the back door. What will I say to her? 'Hi.'

Yes, good start. No, 'hello.' We used to say 'hello' to each other. I remember now.

My grandmother is shaking her head at me and muttering in that ancient, native tongue of hers. What is she saying? Watch the pursed lips, hear the forgotten sounds, a slow recognition in the dim corners of my brain.

Yi qia ngo xiao di.

So that's how it is, she is saying to me, grimly. As if she can read my secret thoughts. That's how it is.

I am scrambling to decode, interpret. Scrambling to form the stilted, guttural sounds in my mouth, to form my own replies. It's a struggle. But all conversations are like this — treading the shaky line between the fluent and effluent. But I am lost. I don't quite know what she is saying, doing my best to piece her words together, from gesture and the odd familiar phrase.

O go kai ge nin kin ding si ngo.

And my mother begins to cry.

I am alarmed, but still half-guessing. Her shaky voice becomes more unbearable. Look into her eyes. Her glance, a blow inside me.

Ngen kin ding yi lai ngo fen le mong ngo!

And now I know what she is saying, finally. Wipe away your tears. She is asking for a promise.

I pause for a moment to see if she is joking or if she is not.

But of course I know she is not.

'Yes,' I say then, quietly, and I will be here.

***

Sustained applause.

That is what's missing these days, I think, as I watch Clare bow before the microphone. And the audience claps, of course, because why not?

In the backstage darkness, I spot Nelson in the corridor, arms folded, watching her. I walk deliberately towards him so he will hear my leathery footsteps and turn to greet me. His eyes narrowing in an effort to place me apart from all the forgotten faces. Ah, spark of recognition. He's got it, he knows me.

'Hey man,' I say.

He returns the greeting, stretching it out into a half-chuckle. 'He-h-eyyy.'

Take his hand, shake it, so the both of you don't have to stand there looking like fools.

'Thought you'd left for good,' he says.

'I did.'

'And now you're back, huh?'

'Just for a few days.'

'Ah.'

A pause is only awkward if you make it so. One, two, three, okay.

'Not a great turnout tonight,' I say.

'Wellll,' he says, peeking at the audience, 'looks half full to me.'

The smartass.

'How's Sydney, then?' he asks, as if resigned to conversation.

'Oh, fine. The pigeons are the same.'

'What?' he asks.

What I mean is, everywhere I go, there are the pigeons. Loitering, cooing, with nothing better to do than follow me around, from city to city. They are the same pigeons. I'm sure of it, somehow.

'Never mind,' I say, because Nelson doesn't care for pigeons, not unless they are named Clare.

Outside, a smattering of applause. Clare reaches for a glass of water, sips it, sets it back on the stool. She looks sideways, over to where the two of us are standing, and she spots me. Curtsies to me, from across the hall. Her lips slightly parted. That slow revealing smile, which — faraway and under a dim, uncertain light — seems a thing of incalculable beauty. Fickle and finite as a setting sun and as sure to disappear should it be given the chance.

Nelson says, 'She's something, isn't she?'

'Yes.'

I lift my hand to say hi, but she is no longer looking, and I feel I am seeing her all at once, somehow, as if in that slight turn of the chin, I know more of her than I ever had in all our months together and apart.

When one person leaves another, everything they have between them becomes split. Split relationship, split emotion, split dignity, split hairs. Banana split. So on.

And the winner of the whole ordeal, of course, is the person who ends up with the most of what you owned together. TV, jewellery, books, crockery. I got the couch, she got Nelson. A fair trade, I guess.

'Clare's taken,' he says to me, this bastard waiting in the wings, 'so if you're thinking about swooping back in and...'

'Shut up,' I say, and he does.

Look at her out there, out of reach, out of grasp. Watch her closely, her body, her face and arms and legs, all of it. Like some distant galaxy one might know and recognise through landmark and feature and familiar shape: notice the arched eyebrow. See the upturned nose. Here, the long hair existing in careful tangles. And there, the milky white skin.

Doradus Nebula. Canis Major. Seyfert's Sextet.

Remember it intimately, or not at all, and never again.

Nelson says something, which I do not catch.

'Sorry?'

'I *said*,' Nelson juts his chin toward my suit, my tie, my button shirt, 'what's with the outfit?'

'Oh. It was a... black tie event,' I say.

'Ah. I was gonna say. You look dressed for a funeral,' he chuckles, and I laugh also.

We listen to her smoky voice outside, trailing off into whistles and applause. I lower my eyes to the sodden dirt still clinging to my shoes. Remember earlier today, in the cemetery, when they lowered my father's limp body into the terrible ground and I was struck by this strange urge to just clap, clap, clap.

'I have to go,' I say.

'Why'd you leave her?'

I look at him for a very long time and then I put my hands in my pockets and walk slowly away to the exit that must be there in all this darkness.

***

Saturday night oozes into Sunday morning.

The muted clap of hymn books closing. Hands folded in prayer. And then a lecture by a man in strange robes, who preaches love and tolerance and other impossible things.

Our sleepy congregation.

Stare at the backs of people's heads and wonder at the things to be found inside: lustful thoughts, painful memories squirreled away, screwdrivers, oven toasters, pomegranates — it's a mystery. Everyone does this staring, I notice. Everyone except those unlucky few who sit in the front rows, who must stare, instead, at their hands, or their knees or else some other empty space where God might reside.

I used to play around this church, on long-ago Sunday afternoons, waiting for my parents to finish with their pious duties and lock the place up. I used to run through the empty pews, my arms forming the wings of an aeroplane or majestic bird. Footsteps echoing off the walls, so that as I trotted to the lectern, eyes tightly shut, it seemed there are many of us, running this way and that. And approaching the curtains which hung, magnificently, from the ceiling to the ground. Stately and foreboding and the colour of clotted blood. I remember peering behind the veneer, running my hands forlornly on the dull coloured brick behind, and letting out a tiny sigh. I don't know what else I was expecting. There was no one behind the curtain.

Stifle a yawn, listen to the same old sermon. Everything as I left it, though some things are new: new bibles, new carports, new carpets, new parishioners. God is still the same, I suppose.

A choir anthem. A prayer.

I make my escape, exiting quietly out the back and through the doors, under a rain-drenched sky. In the shady garden I find a bench to lie across and fall into a gentle sleep. The soft rain dripping through the eaves, come to anoint my head and all its invisible wounds.

***

It is after the service, when they have brought out the coffee and tea and all the assorted knick-knacks. I am approached and greeted by a friendly face whose name I have forgotten, so it is up to me to raise my eyebrows in return and hope it enough to pass as recognition. Mrs Smith, I think she is, or Mrs Wong. How am I to know for sure?

'Robert,' she greets me, 'how are you holding up?' though I can tell from her crinkled, sympathetic smile she knows exactly how I am holding up and is asking just to fuck with me.

'Great,' I say.

'Oh,' she says, and offers me a lamington, which I take but do not eat. So she mimes the act of eating, hand to mouth, as if I am some kind of idiot who needs reminding.

'A lamington is a tricky proposition,' I explain to her defensively. 'I never know for sure if I will like the damn thing, only that I am often tricked into eating one because I like the way the name sounds. Think about it, lamington, lamington, lamington...'

The woman stares at me, growing uncomfortable. The self sabotage continues.

"*'Lamington*," I will often find myself saying, or "I am eating a lamington", or "I am about to eat a lamington", or "that fellow is such a lamington" and so on and so forth.'

I look at the lamington. This ugly hash of browns and flaky dandruff. I pick it at, discriminately. Finally, the woman leaves under some hurried pretence.

And here is the new pastor, come to accost me. Slapping me on the back, clasping my hand like it is some precious object. This stranger, who insists I call him *father*, although he is not my *father* and never will be.

I eat the fucking lamington.

***

Unzip my fly. Take out my penis. Church urinals are always embarrassing. A vague sense of guilt, as though I am somehow under confession.

I cough, if only to assure myself of my own existence.

The cinderblock walls, an off-white shade. The trough smelling of chlorine and faded childhood summers. Breathe in deeply, this olfactory reminiscence, become engulfed in memories that return in splashes, in excited screams, in the pitter-patter of feet on slippery concrete sidewalks. Watch the swimmers, their bodies cutting through the water, with elbows and legs ripping from the surface and under again.

I am in the shallow, where the water is more manageable and comes only to my ears, my feet tiptoeing the submerged bottom. There is my mother in the stands, her floppy hat swaying in the wind. She is calling my name. I wave and smile and she looks at me very sternly until I am cowed into returning to higher ground.

Here, the smaller ones are splashing about, looking like the helpless young of sea creatures with matted hair, goggled eyes, flippers attached to feet. And it seems as though our mothers and fathers are of that ancient, primordial race: discoverers of first land, now patiently in the shallows and guiding their half-walking, half-swimming, half-crying children through our own slow adjustments.

A splash, a scream.

A whistle blown from a lifeguard tower, umpire to some chaotic game of which I do not quite know the rules.

I have just learned to float, just the other day, and I am doing it now. It's a crowning achievement. I can feel the others looking to me enviously, my tiny body splayed out like a starfish, rocking the surface of the water. Opening my eyes to watch the sky. Clouds fanning out, a slow procession of stately white. Billowing like a dream.

There is Clare, who is from my school and sits on my bus, and is causing some sort of fuss. She sobs, shakes her head violently, refuses to let go of the pool edge, though she is a silly girl and can already swim. I watch the wet tangles of her hair, a familiar feeling. She is unsure of the memory in her muscles, does not sufficiently trust in their learned instinct. I am concerned too, in my own way, floating here.

It might happen. A person might easily forget this kind of thing, unlearn it perhaps in their sleep, and it is only through some unspoken faith or stupidity that we wake up in a new day, expecting to know how to swim, to speak, to live.

It's a concern of mine. The unlearning of things.

My fingers prune. Lips turn sky blue. I feel the arms of my father in the water, engulfing me, lifting. Quiet tears of exhaustion. My little body wrapped in a damp blanket, prone as a gunnysack and nestling against his broad shoulder. Ear to his body: listen to the secret heartbeat within, lullaby to a drifting sleep. Blurred sensation of mother kissing my forehead. Quiet murmur of adult voices. Unruly hair swaying before my eyes with each step, step, step to the car.

With the low rays of dusklight that flicker into my eyelids and my dreams, I know, somehow, with unshakeable, childish certainty: that if I open my eyes in the here and now, I would see in every moment those countless others that lie, past and future. The hidden layers of a canvas.

And so what am I to do, of course, but to shut my eyes as tight as I can, block it all out and bury my tear-stained face into his shoulder. His arms which ferry me through this gentle passage high above the earth, softening the shock and bounce of the world, and come to carry me away.

Untitled

Raymond Baltas

and dust
and dust is all,
as all is dust
just as all is left

but be reasonable before
you let breath slip
on dust
that's settled

stirring's dangerous
when feeling's involved
or was

walking weeks on end
with nothing but
ties years-old
now past

— in mind
and in sleep

with hearts a yearning
for when hearts were afire,
still,

and still it's all unrequited
just like then,
still.

I'd hoped for us or 'them'
as we were
to meet a better end

but as it were
time unfurled and
we awoke from our
siamese dream

and just as all is dust,
all is left.

Swimming

Christopher Roche

Swimmers who have just finished their laps have a habit of perching, bird-like, at the end of their lane and gazing distantly over the surface of the water in a sort of spiritual calm. They sit, natural endorphins gliding under the surface of their skin, waiting to dry off a little and regenerate the energy required to change back into their real-world clothes. Perhaps the reason that they remain in this zen-like state for so long is because they are none too keen to experience the feeling of wet skin on underpants, which cling to the thighs like reluctant children and roll up as one awkwardly tries to force them on.

Katie was sitting at the end of the Grand Hotel's fifty-metre pool staring absently across it. She watched the water constantly rippling, allowing herself to become mesmerised by its mingling of blue and turquoise and the flickering of light. Her towel felt cool and damp around her neck, but her conservative one piece swim-suit was beginning to feel like an unwelcome and slimy skin that needed to be shed.

Katie knew that something was missing. It wasn't a case of anything being wrong, in fact on paper everything looked incredibly good. When she wrote or spoke to friends she was aware that they imagined she had the time of her life, all the time. On being introduced to new acquaintances she assumed a false energy which would no doubt give them the same impression.

Katie had experienced moments that many people could only dream of and encountered characters and shared times with them that she would remember for the rest of her life. She had been to places where she'd felt completely overwhelmed, at peace and, essentially, happy. The problem was that having been given these transcendental moments everything in between felt empty. She felt a nothingness, a 'lostness' which she could never define or release. At times it felt like a shadow which was always behind her, but whenever she turned to look directly at it, it would swing in the other direction and she could spend a lifetime trying to spin around like a dog and never truly glimpse it. So how would she find an answer to a problem that didn't rationally exist but which she felt was there? Her treatment so far was to ignore it, to 'man up' and pretend to everyone she met that she had the happiest life in the world.

A man in his early twenties pulled himself out of the water with one strong movement of his muscular physique. He walked over and snatched up his towel from the adjacent bench, the water shimmering as the sun fell on his perfectly formed stomach. Aware that she was openly staring at him, Katie snapped herself out of her reverie with a blink and a quick movement of her head. Her heart raced dispropor-tionately as she fought the temptation to look back and see if he had noticed. For someone with such outward confidence, she thought, she could be so inwardly uncool. When she did steal a guilty glance he was staring straight at her. He smiled a modest yet knowing smile one could fall in love with in a moment. Katie, annoyed but utterly subject to her shyness, stood up and gathered her bag clumsily before walking briskly across the warm tiles and into the relative safety of the women's changing room.

Katie was stunningly beautiful. She had thick, rich chocolate hair which was lucky, because had she been such a strikingly attractive blonde, people might have overlooked her abnormal intellect. She had a level of intelligence which many men found intimidating, something that she could read instantly because of a keen attention to detail and an instinctive ability to interpret people's expressions. Despite this she was modest. She was intelligent enough to realise the fleeting nature of everything that she possessed. She was aware that she was beautiful and was never under any illusion as to how she was being received in social situations, yet she also knew that her beauty meant nothing and that, at twenty-nine, it was fading. Three years ago she would walk along the beach and everyone's heads would turn. She would walk with the calm confidence of someone completely content with themselves but without (she hoped and, naturally, assumed) making others feel diminished in her presence. Now she was becoming just like everyone else. Other, younger, girls with less cellulite, Hollywood stomachs and that youthful elasticity which no amount of firming lotion can recreate, would steal the attention. It didn't bother her, not really. She knew that she was in a slow, laborious decline and that in five years she would be too old for most men. Naturally, she would prefer that life wasn't like that, but since it was, she accepted it and though this rather gloomy thought might enter her head on occasion, it rarely affected her. She did increasingly find herself taking a slightly vindictive and immature comfort in the knowledge that the twenty-five year old girls who currently enjoyed unlimited attention from keen young men would, before they ever understood what they had, lose their perfect figures and become just another woman who men didn't notice.

As if on cue, a naked old lady was walking around the changing room far more than was necessary, invading Katie's personal space as she shuffled past. Katie had never understood why certain people felt the need to get utterly naked in changing rooms. It was perfectly easy to take your towel, bra and underpants into the shower cubicles and put them on before emerging, and if that was too much effort you could at least have the courtesy to put them on immediately without publicly talcum-powdering your inner thighs and duck-walking around to test that you'd applied enough to avoid chafing.

The woman was now, unbelievably, drying her hair in front of the mirror still entirely naked. Where thigh met buttock her cellulite bulged as if her skin had been sandwiched in a waffle-maker and even from behind it was evident that she had not felt the need to groom for some years. Katie wondered if she would ever end up like that, not caring. In a way she envied the old woman with her wild grey pubic hair and grotesque sagging chest. Here was someone who did not care one bit what anyone thought of her. Incomprehensibly, she was probably happier than Katie who, for all her assets and false felicity, had been unable to find a partner who she could possibly come close to loving. She had given up on the idea of ever being 'in love' again. She had received plenty of advances from a mass of idiots, chauvinists, commitment-phobes and short-back-and-sides, opinionated, puffed up yuppies trying to sell their own particular brew of arrogance, stupidity and insecurity carefully wrapped in a well-packaged exterior designed to mislead the customer into becoming involved in something which promised to be amazing but would always, inevitably, disappoint. It had been nine years since Katie had met a man who had consistently surprised her and whose intentions she hadn't been able to sum up with one word. In fact it continued to baffle her that people could possibly be as boring and simple as they seemed. Time after time, man after man, mediocre date after mediocre date, the male race had failed to perform.

Occasionally Katie had felt that it was almost there, that rare ingredient people often referred to as 'the spark'. If she had been ticking the potential husband boxes there had been plenty of hopefuls who would have fulfilled every criteria, and certainly her friends jumped at the chance to snap up similarly high-scoring life-partners and settled down to a predictable but comfortable life of children and the suburbs. In a way, Katie found these men the most tedious. Good blokes who would give her everything and never be unkind or step out of line. Well behaved, tame, unquestioning men who could never make her heart skip a beat, never make her feel like she was seventeen again and who she could never fall in love with. If that's the answer, if that's happiness, Katie thought, I choose an unhappy life with the hope of moments to restore faith in — but she did not know what the faith was in exactly. She had had this conversation with herself a hundred times and had occasionally confided it to a close friend, but it was now a tired subject and her counterparts were moving on, increasingly focused on their own families and children with all the complex problems and worries which accompanied the life they chose.

As the sliding doors politely opened for her and she stepped out of the hotel lobby into London's crisp spring air she momentarily expected something to happen, to feel different, but as she descended the steps into the city twilight she sighed and walked briskly on, feeling nothing as usual.

Cold Snap

Theodore Ell

If the world is ours then why does the spring night
not have the warmth of one drop of human blood?
It is the same as when we snap our fingers,
drink the sea, let rivers go thirsty for good
and boil the sky dry with the breath of our work:
if nature recoils, we complain, spoilt and rude.

'Nature, who nurtured us, tortures and teases
us,' we grizzle. 'It does just as it pleases
to spite our desires.' If only it were true.
The spring may blow cold but it does not mean to.

The Mending

Barbara Hatten

Jo is walking down her street, indifferent to the insistent drizzle blown diagonal by the wind and soaking her through as if she's just stepped out of the shower. She is as light as she can be, shivering with cold and an excitement that verges on mania. It doesn't get better than this, she thinks, as she bends over an upholstered chair with one leg snapped like a broken sapling, tracing the lines of the pattern on the wet upholstery with a shaking finger.

The chair crowns a pile of household debris on the nature strip; stained blinds, a rusty heater, the metal tub of an old washing machine dotted with holes like a sieve, a cheap plastic chair still intact. Jo imagines sitting on the plastic chair outside, warming her hands over a wood fire in the tub, converted into a brazier, sparks leaping from the writhing orange flames into the darkness, and afterwards, eating her dinner inside on the other chair, dry now, and with its fourth leg glued back on, as sturdy as it ever was. She looks up. It's almost council clean-up day, and all along the street, in the drizzle illuminated by the streetlights, is pile after pile of junk, each with its own special secrets to be discovered. She hurries back home to get the truck. There will be no time to change out of her wet clothes, because she will not be the only one searching by dawn.

No wonder the neighbours call me The Scavenger, she thinks, momentarily grim as she surveys her back yard in the dim light.

There is a truck parked in the corner, and the rest of it resembles a wrecker's, grass inching up hopefully through the meagre spaces not yet covered with stuff. I'm a Hoarder too. Wish I were a Fixer.

She can see the beauty, or at least the possibility of utility in all of it, from the tiny bag of assorted nails and screws thrown carelessly on the back step, to her most recent find, a weather-damaged wooden boat minus the motor with 'free-to-good-home' painted on the side, sitting on bricks patiently awaiting her attention.

Jo remembers Luke wandering around the stuff when she brought home her first load, picking up an old barbeque grate and frowning at it, then putting it down again, running his hand along a battered table top, his long hair flame-red, his hands pale against the dark wood.

The barbeque grate is long gone, the table mended, carefully sanded, stained, varnished and occupying the living room. She can't sit there alone, preferring to eat in front of the television. She has too many memories of meals, of games, of the two of them pushing a laughing baby back and forth across the polished surface. Jo wrenches the door of the truck open and climbs in, the engine spluttering into life on the third attempt. She coaxes the truck down the driveway like a reluctant child, and eases it onto the road, pulling up beside a row of boxes laden with waterlogged books.

Luke was both a Fixer of broken things and a minimalist who discarded, sold or gave away anything they didn't use. In those respects he was good for her for a time, so that her disorderliness remained an interior thing, invisible to others, and contained within the boundaries of her own mind, like a wild beast safely imprisoned within its cage. When she lost Luke and their son Charlie to the road that ran straight past her front door, the bars of the cage fell away, and the beast went on the prowl for all to see, so that sometimes the shame of it makes her want to disappear still.

Under the paperback crime fiction, which Jo loves, and resolves to dry later, she finds a set of leather bound classics, wrapped safely in plastic; books by the Brontë sisters, Dickens, the complete works of Shakespeare. They smell of old paper, and the editions date back to the 1930s. She places them carefully on the front seat, not daring to explore them further in her damp state, and keeps going until the truck is packed and the street is full of cars driving slowly, stopping and starting with their headlights ghostly in the rain, while men with umbrellas sift through the piles like discerning shoppers.

Back home, Jo soaks awhile in the bath, and heads to bed for the few hours before she has to get ready for work. She can unpack later. It has been too long since she washed her grimy sheets, and she slips into them gingerly, resolving to do it soon. Trawling for junk is easy, but she baulks at the tasks of daily living, beyond those required to get to work and back.

She is surprised to wake up in the late morning feeling hopeful as the sun and wind burst in through the window together like a pair of excitable boys nudging her out of her warm sleepy stupor, her tangle of sheets, as if to say, get up, get up, because today can be different to all the other days if you'll only let it be so. She sits up in bed and regards herself critically in the mirror. Once she had looked tousled in a deliberately sexy, mysterious way in the mornings that had driven Luke to grab her from behind and wrestle her back down onto the bed laughing. She can't imagine anyone doing that now to the woman in the mirror with her puffy, black shadowed eyes, her brown paper skin and her unfashionably long grey hair.

'Get yourself ready for work, Medusa,' she says slowly and carefully to the Mirror Woman. Her voice sounds like it could do with a squirt from an oilcan, croaky as it is from disuse. She talks when she has to at work, but not much anywhere else. Mirror Woman cracks a smile, even winks at her in an apparent display of wholehearted approval, the sun framing her hair in a grey fuzzy felt halo.

Jo walks briskly along the cracked lino floors of the nursing home, breathes in the faint whiff of urine, and tends to Mrs Sloane with her sagging, failing body and her fogged-up mind.

'Do you know, dear,' says Mrs Sloane from her wheelchair as Jo bunches up her stockings to ease them over her gnarled, arthritic feet. 'Do you know that my two daughters haven't been to see me for a very long time? Every day I wait for them and they don't come.'

Jo feels the bathroom tiles hard and cold beneath her knees as she looks into Mrs Sloane's face, inhabited for once.

'I'm sure they will come soon,' she lies, slipping away from the older woman's grief as if skating along the tiles. 'Perhaps they've been busy, or they've gone away for a holiday.'

'They might take me out for lunch one day. I'd love that.'

Mrs Sloane's hands are rubbing, one against the other, like dry autumn leaves tumbling to the ground in the wind.

'The food here is awful, and the people are so dreary. They don't converse you know. I'm lucky to have you to talk to.'

Jo straps on the old lady's shoe, then brushes her hair with gentle strokes, the way she would like her own hair brushed. She puts Mrs Sloane's feet gently back on the wheelchair, and pushes her up to the dining room, where the diversional therapist reads the day's news enthusiastically without switching off the television. There is an item about a lost child. The kitchen staff bring out the lukewarm breakfasts, and she prepares to feed Reg, who was once a government minister. When it is time to leave, she breaks all the rules and kisses Mrs Sloane goodbye.

As soon as Jo gets home, she sheds her uniform like a caterpillar wriggling out of a chrysalis. She rummages through the few remaining clean clothes on the bed, chooses jeans and a top too good for scavenging, so she won't be tempted, ties her hair back, packs a toothbrush and change of clothes in case. She has a week off anyway, was planning to spend it tackling the mess outside, but hell, that won't go anywhere. She pulls everything out of the truck, chucks it into the black hole in the garage, except for the classics from the rubbish heap. She decides to take them with her, as a talisman. This time the truck roars into life with an unusual enthusiasm that seems to match her own and she sets off past the diminished piles, past the private contractors chucking them into a truck, around the bend and into the slow moving traffic of a late weekday afternoon.

She's halfway to Queensland before she stops, pulling into the cement car park of a roadside motor inn at two in the morning, so grateful to the bleary eyed man who answers the night bell she wants to embrace him.

She loves the bland, neat room, the absence of chaos, the clean sheets and the properly made bed. She'd like to stay for a while, have someone look after her for a change, but there's no time for that now. She sleeps better than she ever does at home, then breakfasts on white squares of toast with spreads in little plastic containers and coffee that tastes like dishwater, puts one Vegemite and one honey container in her bag for the road, then springs back into the driver's seat with the energy of a teenager.

It isn't until she's nearly at the border that she thinks about what she is doing and pulls over. Doubt and fear overwhelm her until she's about ready to turn back. She gets out and walks around in long grass strewn with rubbish, talks herself through it.

'What if they don't want to see me? I'll turn around and drive back. Won't have lost anything except money. What if they aren't there? Same.'

A kindly man in his seventies parks his Commodore behind the truck to offer help. He rolls down the window and yells at her with the engine running.

'You okay, love?'

'I'm fine thanks. Just about to get back on the road.'

He pulls out straight away. She walks slowly back to the truck, gets in and grips the wheel with one hand, turns on the ignition with the other.

'Last chance to change your mind, babe.'

She doesn't, and she's there in no time at all.

She remembers the way from years ago and going over and over it in her memory. Half an hour from the highway, down a succession of narrow tree-shaded bitumen roads winding up and down steep hillsides, past paddocks lush from the recent rain. She turns off at a collection of letterboxes, makes it down all ten kilometres of the rattling and shaking dirt without getting bogged, and pulls up at the gate. Her shoulders feel like rocks, her heart thuds against her ribcage, and her mouth is dry. She forces herself to get out, open the gate, drive through, get out, swing it closed, lifting it over the uneven ground. There is some comfort in this small ritual.

Just a few hundred metres more and she parks near the house, a weatherboard, freshly painted, surrounded by frangipani in flower, and a well-tended veggie garden fenced off to the side. Chooks wander contentedly around a large enclosure on the edge of the garden. Luke's old Holden HQ ute is parked in the shed, next to another, sleeker modern car. Could Charlie be driving already? Everything is in order as usual. There is no clutter. She plucks a frangipani flower from the tree nearest the front door and puts it in her hair, then knocks on the open door, peering through the screen to a long hallway with polished floors leading to the sunlit veranda out the back. The shower is running. She waits, knowing they have heard, perhaps seen her coming, and have chosen to take their time to emerge.

Luke comes, then, and swings the screen door open, barefoot, wrapped in a faded sarong, his hair longer, his face more lined than she remembers. He leans casually against the doorjamb, his expression inscrutable.

'Why now?' he asks, cold, his arms folded. She sees his shaking hands, his attempt to still them. 'Why did you come now? Why not phone first? Why not write or email, or send a card on your son's birthday?'

Jo is thrown. She has never seen this in Luke before, this naked hostility.

'One of the old ladies I look after,' she stammered. 'She doesn't see her daughters. So I thought it was important to visit Charlie.' She is inarticulate with a misery that weighs on her chest and makes it hard to breathe. 'I'm sorry. I shouldn't have come.' She turns as the tears spill over and begin to run down her cheeks.

She is resolved. She will return to her junk and her work. She will fill up all the empty spaces somehow. She will try to find a Fixer of people who can help her sift through the stiff and rusty parts of her so that she can be of more use, at least to herself.

Luke follows her, calls her back.

'Wait! At least have the decency to say hello to Charlie. I'm tired of trying to justify your complete absence in his life.'

She turns and sees a woman standing behind him in the doorway.

The woman has a strong, sweet face, and a forehead wrinkled with concern.

The woman smiles at her, a smile that wavers at the edges.

'You must be Charlie's mum. I'm Diana. Come in and have a cup of tea. He's at a friend's place, but he should be home any moment.'

Jo obediently follows them out to the veranda, sits, tense in the morning sun, and accepts tea and biscuits. Luke gazes resolutely at the tree-lined creek down the hill. He will not look at her. Diana asks her polite questions about her journey, about where she lives, her work.

Jo remembers lying next to Luke on the beach in the afternoon, both of them trying to read for a thesis in literature, then swimming, laughing in sparkling clear water, slippery like porpoises. Then they were just a pair of promising students with a bright future. So much was given, and then taken away.

'I didn't think I'd ever be able to work,' she says. 'I take my medication now, see the shrink regularly, manage the house more or less. I'm still a bowerbird. I used to drive Luke mad.'

She is unravelling now, the words spilling out too fast, as she twists her skirt around and around her fingers, first one way, then the other.

'We were happy together at first, until I got sick. I had myself convinced that Luke and Charlie would be better off without me. So I managed to persuade Luke that I'd be better off without them. Probably it wasn't true, but I was getting sicker and sicker, and I couldn't bear the effect it was having on both of them, watching the light going out of their eyes the way I knew it had gone out of mine. I was struggling to understand what was real and what wasn't and I wasn't really sure of anything. I wanted to die.

'I didn't have any reason to believe I'd get better and I told Luke that. Luke couldn't cope with the idea I'd changed permanently, and I kept telling him to take Charlie and leave. How was he to know I didn't mean it? So he took me to hospital one last time, and when I came out, he was gone.

'My parents stepped in and took over. They thought for a long time that it was their fault I was so ill, especially my mum.'

Diana smiles a wry smile.

'I have a grown up daughter, Jo. We mothers are experts at guilt, aren't we?'

Jo looks at her, and Diana breaks away from her gaze, becomes enamoured with the view, as if to snap shut right there the book of her own life. Jo waits a moment, and then decides to continue. She has seen therapists do this often, slip uncomfortably close to self disclosure, as if stepping to the edge of a cliff, and then withdraw, perhaps regain control of the encounter with another question. After all, she has always been the patient.

'My parents didn't like to waste anything. They were frugal, careful to make things last, like most of their generation. They didn't expect me to take it to such extremes. They've both passed away now.'

Jo stands up and begins to pace. Luke is watching her intently now. For a few moments the sun escapes from behind clouds, lights up the grey sky and illuminates the grassy paddocks below them to a brilliant green, before the clouds push insistently in front of it again and dull its power.

'Luke let me stay in the house, even though it had belonged to his parents. It was his family home. I'll always be grateful to him for that.'

They had all loved that house, with its pressed ceilings and bay windows, its farm-sized back yard, its long, happy family history that stretched back for generations. Without it she'd have ended up on the streets probably, filthy, vulnerable, laden with plastic bags and old newspapers.

'I came to visit for a while, but it was too hard for all of us to move on, so I stopped coming. I'm a lot better now, and I thought it was time to come back. Besides, I have a present for Charlie.'

Luke takes Diana's hand, but he is looking at Jo.

'You know I did truly believe you wanted us to go.' He changes position, as if to shift a burden. 'I'd lost hope.'

Jo nods. She hasn't ever blamed him. She isn't sure what she'd have done in the same circumstances. He has to live with the decisions he made at the time just as she does. She is relieved he is no longer angry about her long absence. She has no doubt now that Charlie would have been better off with a mad mother than no mother at all. It's too late to change the past though, and she hasn't become bitter, only more anxious, eccentric and lonely.

She is flooded with memories. Charlie, at two, rugged up like an Eskimo, laughing and laughing and begging for more when they played one-two-three jump with him on a long bushwalk. Coming home to a silent house after hospital that last time, medicated to the eyeballs, as clear in the head as she'd ever been, but not trusting it, so not calling them back, even though she felt as empty as the house.

They sit in silence for a while, the three of them, listening to a swelling chorus of frogs. The clouds are heavy with rain, likely to fall soon and chill the air, sending them indoors. Jo wants the others, along with Charlie to be her family now. She longs for it as for a mother, but she isn't sure it's possible. If something is broken into too many pieces, there are bound to be jagged edges when it is put back together. The mending takes patience and skill and it doesn't always work.

Jo wipes her eyes and nose on a hanky Diana gives her, walks back out to the truck and pulls out the bag of books, just as a battered combie comes up the drive too fast. She stands there with the books in her hand, watches her son — her tall beautiful son with his boy's features turning into a man's — unfurl himself from the small space of the driver's seat and stroll towards her, shaking his head as if trying to wake from a dream.

'Mum,' he says in an adult's voice that will take some getting used to. 'Where have you been?'

He thanks her politely for the books. She doesn't know if he will even read them, whether books are a part of his life as they have always been a part of his father's, a part of hers. She hugs him and he is stiff in her arms, but it doesn't matter because he lets her do it.

She steps back to look at him, to talk, but the words have dried up for both of them, and they don't know where to start. For a moment she sees herself through his eyes — middle-aged, unfashionably dressed, a little dishevelled, odd looking. She aches for him, for herself, for Mrs Sloane, for the lost years. All the aching goes away when he grabs her hand to lead her back into the house, and she hopes that perhaps it isn't too late after all to mend what was broken.

The House by the Mouth of the River

Lauren Arcamone

Last night I dreamed of picking flowers in the field again. Shaded by the trees, my parents watched and laughed as I ran from flower to flower in the grey autumn sun. I heard only fragments of their conversation, but I felt their words as a warm blurring of love and sleepiness carried by the breeze. I drifted in and out of daydream. When I looked again, the grass had become filled with treasures of unimaginable worth: rubies, amethysts, opals, all in a sea of peridot green. In the distance, my father's low voice rumbled and my mother laughed in response; a resounding bell of pleasure, warm and full of promise like the spring.

Far out in the open field I came across a sapphire: a bright blue thing of a hundred petals. My eyes lit up like jewels themselves and I moved towards it, slowly, like a hunter towards prey. My mother's voice was lost in the rousing wind, and my father's deep rolling laugh became thunder overhead. I snatched the thing and crushed it to my lips, my nose, and then the ground gave way and I couldn't breathe and I was swallowed by the earth. Then, perhaps, I woke.

This morning the pillow next to mine was cold, as though he'd woken early, or hadn't slept. Often I wake this way. I don't mind, and I don't blame him. It might seem on the surface of things that this is a quiet place, but it isn't at all, not really. The visitors who come here never stay long, yet they are many and ceaseless.

Our home is by the mouth of that old river whose name I forget, and all the ones who journey there stop here first, searching for their guide. I know the way but it isn't my place to take them, and nor would I want to. The way is dark and loveless, the river deep, and I don't think I can swim. He is the one who leads them there safely.

I break my fast on fruit. Each day is the same in this way, and has been ever since I arrived, that first year when the winter came. At meals I sit alone at a long and regal table with high-backed chairs and gold-rimmed goblets. I rarely eat with him, although sometimes he sits with me out of politeness, or perhaps out of love. It's rather hard to tell.

There are no gardens here, but I don't mind, not really. I used to pick flowers all the time, but the idea disturbs me now. They're dead as soon as you snap the stem. There are no birds here either, or if there are, they never sing. In winter there's the wind and that old river, whose name I forget, but little else. I don't mind the wind's music, but the sound of the river bothers me the way a siren would, far away yet constant. Sometimes I think I hear voices in the rushing water, but when I shake my head they're always gone, or smothered by the wind.

My mind finds ways to occupy itself. I drift in and out of daydream, here in his home one minute and laying in a field of flowers the next. Once I thought I heard my mother calling me, crying. Her voice echoed through the fields like a storm as she tore the earth to bloody pieces, calling, crying, searching. The world grew cold and lightless and the peridot grass turned to dust and I woke in a sweat, breathless and buried far beneath the earth and then I woke again, and pinched myself, and heard the rushing water.

He watches while I eat. He watches with the same expression of hunger he wore that first year I arrived, when the winter came and he held a banquet and we were the only ones there. It was a feast fit for a hundred. The table creaked under the weight of golden dishes full-brimming goblets, and We sat, and I ate, and the visitors passed in silence.

I followed him, once, as he led them there, to that old river. Even the sound of it washed my memory clear. I was afraid to look, in case it stole my senses, but he found me just in time. His eyes were bright with love, or with anger. It was rather hard to tell. I wept; that night he came to bed and crushed me to his lips, to his nose, and it felt like being buried. I think I was forgiven.

Last night I dreamed of picking flowers in a field. I killed a bright blue flower when I plucked it from the ground, and then I woke and found his pillow cold. When I slept I found him next to me like he'd never left my side. Somewhere in a dream, I was smothered by the wind and fell apart in a hundred petals, and then perhaps I woke, or then perhaps I didn't. A bird in a cage cannot tell how many walls extend beyond her bars. Dreams make for uncertain prisons

That first year, when the winter came, he said he wanted me to stay forever. Though he'd lain a banquet, all it took was that one fruit. Though the seeds were bitter, I came back all the same.

I break my fast on fruit. The visitors come and go. Although they are many they make no noise. Each day is exactly the same in this way, and has been ever since that first year I arrived, when the ground gave way and I was swallowed by the earth.

A flower will die as soon as you snap the stem, but I was different. There are no birds here and of course I shouldn't be surprised. This place is underground; no living thing dares near it. But still I wake at night convinced that if I close my eyes and open them again the sunlight will appear and winter will be over, and at last I will hear my mother's voice, warm and full of promise like the spring.

Moon, She a Coin

Amelia Walkley

A fingerprint of some bejewelled deity,

dusked with milk

a golden seal, pressed and stamped, fastening the inked envelope
of sky

some prestigious mark.

Moon, she a coin; the sky a sorry purse

smattered with shrapnel-stars

currencies of the overworlds, gilt cosmos merchants a-bartering

in suns and spheres, comets and planets

tossed like dice in the she-universe, an orb of trade

yes, the celestials tender value yet...

Summer Is

Amelia Walkley

Summer is
a bowl of cherries red.
Tooth pierces plump fruit
and juice weeps from the wound
to trickle down my thumb
and seep beneath my nails
staining my lips with its scarlet taint.
Stones are discarded along with poker-green stalks
but the thought lingers.
This summer's taste
is yet sweet upon my wet mouth.

The Redness of Red

Rachel Olding

Then God said, 'let there be light'; and there was light.
(Genesis 1:3)

At first, the undulations are miniscule. A tremble. Like a heart rate monitor as the patient slowly ceases breathing, it is almost a straight line. The wavelength stretches further. It is just decipherable. It stretches 380 mm. It stretches 480 mm. It is a rollercoaster now. Up, down, up, down. The wavelength stretches further, 580 mm, 680 mm. It is unmistakable, piercing through the light. At 760 mm it can go no further — the furthest point of the electromagnetic spectrum. It quivers. Perhaps it is nervous; the sun has absorbed every other colour but not this one. This one was reflected. One chance only. It tremors. Please! I can't go any further.

The retina! Oh! The retina. The first set of nervous fibres is punctured by the wave. Excruciatingly. It feels like electrocution. But everything is alight, alive. The fibre is stimulated. It dances all the way up the optic nerve to the brain.

And behold, the deep hue emerges.

Red.

Crimson, Alizarin, Carmine, Brazilin, Scarlet, Vermilion, Maroon, Ruby, Dahlia, Burgundy. From the Archaic Homo sapiens whose earliest pigment was red ochre, to the Cro-Magnons' cave paintings, to the Germanic *rauduz*, the Indo-European *roudh*, the Old English *read* and the Middle English *reed*. It denoted roses and the blood-reddened cross, the edges of a sword, the luminosity of flames, fire and lightning, dawn and sunset, the pigments and dyes of the human body, the skin and lips, hair and beards, cloth and garments, blood, coral, rose, ruby, grapes, wine, ripe wheat, soil and earth.

It grows from being mere radiant stimuli in light to become an arbitrary linguistic sign and then a colour with psychological and emotional meaning. It is the battle between life and death. The curtains of death close in and, along with all the bland greys and browns, a different colour is added to the scene. When the blow is delivered, the artery bursts and a new colour sprays through the air. Red. Blood. The most powerful colour the human race is heir to. Many are adamant that blood is polysemous, that every subsequent symbol traces back to the archetypal experience of red blood.

It came to represent bloodshed, war and struggle and was inherited as a symbol of death and suffering. Heroic figures are given the honour of red dress in Japan. At the dawn of the twentieth century, the Bolshevik Party created a flag to represent the Communist movement. It had to represent the workers' struggle against the perilous capitalist class. It was red. From this came the red menace, the red peril, the Red Army, and then, Red China led by Mao Zedong — the Red Sun.

But new life cannot continue without blood streaming through its veins. In India, the bride wears red as she stands at the threshold of posterity. The blood pumps harder. With every circle of the anatomy it must pass the gatekeeper — the heart. Thump, thump. As the blood runs faster it congests the primary sexual organs. Lust, love, sexuality, intimacy, fertility. A rush of blood to the head; it swarms the face and swamps every pore. Embarrassment, anger, panic, hatred, uncontrollable passion. The most intense emotions known to humans are blood-curdling.

Red is a matrix of inherited, learned, semantic, sensory and natural allegories. The precise origin of symbols remains a mystery, a guessing game of metonyms solidified in time and blind metaphoric mapping. Perhaps it is physiological. As the longest wavelength, red appears closest. It stands out in relation to all other hues by virtue of heightened saturation and brightness. Red, simply, is the most colour. It relays danger and grabs our attention before any other colour. But the quest to whittle the redness of red down to a physiological reaction continues to evade us.

'Can we reduce it to the firing of a few brain cells?' Dr Colin Clifford from the University of Sydney froths at the thought. 'If we can reduce experience to physiology then what would that physiology look like and what would it really mean to say that my experience of the redness of red corresponds to the firing of a few brain cells?' As the experience of red becomes mechanised, machines are being created. Technicians chip away at a machine that can recognise a cherry and pick it, feel the surface tension, judge the intensity of its deep crimson colour and know that it must have a hint of purple to be perfect. Or collect the unspoilt grapes to make that red, red wine. They are barely in their infancy but every day, as physiologists hunt down that ephemeral experience of red, they are closer to completion.

Dr Clifford's room and its contents are bland and grey. Even the overcast sky blankets the room in a depressing light. He wears a brown t-shirt and rests his hands on the sterile grey table. There is not a glimpse of colour. But his eyes bulge as he talks of red like a far-away utopia. 'We really don't have much understanding of the physiological links between colours and emotions. We've got good ideas of what's going on in the brain's early stages of the visual system, in the eye and the retina as the signal gets relayed back to the brain. Once things get to the brain we're really only just starting to understand that process.'

And what hope do you have of decoding that, when there are people like myself? Just as you edge closer to tracing those wires through the brain, here I am with complete cross-wiring. I mightily beat my head about a visible object, for so long I tried to understand these lights and colours which often come my way. And only now do I understand scarlet. What is scarlet? It is like the sound of a trumpet. It is the letter R, the number 8. Sometimes B and X and 3 but they are bright red. G is red but it's rusty, not so intense, kind of dull, it's hard to explain. I see it in my head, it's just there, like an extra sensation.

He is a synesthete [colour grapheme]. Male; 5'9"; twenty-six years old. Senses: cross-wired.

I am really good at remembering names. I think of the first letter of their name and that colour sticks with me. Friday is a red day, why is that? I don't know. I play a lot of pool and the numbers and letters of the balls are all wrong. But I've been playing for so many years now that it's sort of toned it down. But my colours never change, maybe slightly over a long time, but every synesthete has different colours and they are always consistent. My girlfriend and I play a lot of scrabble. I pick up an X and red swarms the back of my mind. Red — ten points!

Cause of synesthesia: Unknown.

Perhaps every child has synesthesic linking in their brain but it gets pruned back as most people get older. Over time we learn that 'A' is not always red, as it was on the alphabet chart at school or the fridge magnets at home. But this does not explain why, for some synesthetes, red has a scent and a taste. Perhaps it is a hereditary or completely random genetic disposition. Perhaps pathways between the auditory and visual areas in the brain continue to exist beyond neoteny so that the visual cortex is stimulated when the auditory is. Research has been slow because there is no threat. Synesthetes are normal, they use their parallel senses to their advantage, they tend to have excellent memories and prefer order and symmetry. It can get in the way of cognitive development — poor maths, right-left confusion, more prone to unusual experiences like déjà vu and a sense of portentousness. Red can be eerily intense. Even frightening.

And for me? The synesthete pains to describe, in every minute detail, the full crimson red he pictures when he hears the D sharp two octaves above middle C. But I look at a sunset and see one bland red. Quite bright, very intense, but just red. Put five red cards in front of me, each of a different shade, and they all look the same. Your eyes are sensitive to big differences, mine are not. I wanted to join the Army Reserves but had to give up the dream. But it's all good, it makes for a good story at the pub. I lose count of the number of time I've nearly run a red light. Amber, red, orange, earthy red, magenta, it's all the same. I lose count of the number of times I've come home with unripe tomatoes, damn it.

He is partially colour blind. Hereditary. Male; 5'8"; twenty-two years old. On the tiny Micronesian atoll of Pingelap, 4597 kilometres away, the intensity of red is all but absent. What is it like to live without red? Or be part of a people where an entire culture of colour might be missing? Typhoon Lengeiki in 1775: ninety per cent of the Pingelapese die. Just twenty survivors. But one is an achromatope — complete colour blindness. They are extremely fertile. The population reaches one hundred after a few decades. By the fourth generation achromatopsia is entrenched. It affects ten per cent, one in twelve as opposed to one in 30,000 for the rest of the world. One-third are carriers. Myths swarm the small island: a pregnant woman whose unborn child was blinded by the blazing sun; a Christian minister whose children were cursed due to his lack of evangelical zeal; an extramarital affair in which the ruler's wife, Dokas, and the god of Pingelap, Isopaw, gave birth to two affected children; and Pingelapese forced to work in German phosphate mines in Nauru who returned to father achromatopes. By the age of four the achromatopes cannot see finer detail; they squint their eyes in the face of bright light and cannot distinguish colour. But somehow, they have a sort of theoretical knowledge and know-how, a comprehensive hypertrophy of curiosity and memory in the absence of perception. They learn to compensate cognitively for what they cannot directly perceive. They can't see red, but they know red.

Over 13,000 kilometres away, men from all corners of the world pace up and down the main canal of De Wallen in downtown Amsterdam. They peruse the storefront rooms, each lit-up with a neon red light, each with a lingerie-clad woman offering her services. Welcome to Amsterdam's red-light district. Flickering, dusty red lights used to litter the Boys Towns of Mexico, red paper lanterns hang outside Dashilan brothels in China, railway workers used to leave glass lanterns outside Bangkok's Patpong parlours in case they needed to be quickly located, gaudy neon lights beckon bikies and backpackers in Sydney's Kings Cross. The lure of the red light. The lure of a herring fish, caught in the North Sea and the Baltic in the nineteenth century and smoked over a fire until it turns a dark brownish-red; its strong smell would confuse hounds chasing foxes. They would track down the hypnotising smell. Only for it to be a red herring.

She can do more than smell it or know it or be lured by its bright tincture. She can *see* red with her third eye. She looks at the human body. She sees the aura, the entire electro-magnetic field surrounding the body. Like a divine encounter, it radiates out from the body in seven different coloured rays. The body is in rainbow equilibrium. Without red, the balance is tipped.

She sees a black spot. It covers the red ray — the colour of construction. It could be a problem with many things, she says. Red blood cells, the liver, blood pressure. But now she knows where to focus. She follows in the footsteps of the Ancient Egyptian god Thoth, Aristotle and his disciple Avicenna, the famous renaissance healer Paracelsus, and the modern day chromotherapist Rudolf Steiner. She will project red light to restore a deficiency. It will stimulate blood circulation, energise the body and increase blood pressure. She will suggest increasing everyday exposure to red. Drink water exposed to red rays, eat red meat and vegetables, add red spices to meals, meditate on red, find a red jasper or garnet stone, even some Myrrh. Nothing happens in the physical body unless it first happens in the etheric body, she says. Cells need colour vibration. The pituitary gland comes into play when exposed to red. It sends a chemical sign to release adrenaline. Don't paint the walls of a jail red though. It encourages violence, anger, distress, hyperactivity, neurosis and aggression. It speeds up blood pressure and breathing. Be careful, she says, red can be very powerful. It is life and death, a flickering wavelength, sight and blindness, a strange lure, sometimes inexplicable intensity.

Who would have known that little wild poppy could have a red so sudden it made my blood stop?

Dreaming (A Palindrome)

Lauren Arcamone

Apocalypse dreaming —

is she dreaming awake or dreaming?

Thousands of galaxies dying, centuries crumbling, memories
  lost.

In waking —

a leaden tongue, a flesh heavy with mortality,

dreaming of release.

The bright becoming dark,

warm becoming cold,

light becoming weight.

Escape with unravelling and aching curses,

bitter and abusing the mouth

that forms her fading landscape,

the sunken becoming life.

Imagine: to escape this for aching and aching —

escape to worlds of millions and millions of dreamers,

and she

creates,

she, and

dreamers of millions and millions of worlds. To escape aching,
  and aching —

for this escape: to imagine

life becoming sunken,

the landscape fading her forms that mouth the abusing and
  bitter curses, aching and unravelling

with escape.

Weight becoming light,

cold becoming warm,

dark becoming bright

(the release of dreaming).

Mortality with heavy flesh, a tongue leaden,

a-waking in lost memories, crumbling centuries,

dying galaxies of thousands...

dreaming or awake?

Dreaming.

She is dreaming apocalypse.

Pardon the Scherzo

Theodore Ell

Once an unsuccessful cynic
(it might have been me) stooped to say,
'Musicians don't like most music —
only the bit they're trying to play.'

Thoughtlessness is the source of wrongs
and that is the case with this one,
for those who make life of songs
when not presenting them, listen.

If our cynic ever forgets
this, let him go deaf. There would be
more music and fewer regrets.
Musicians, explore. Set him free.

Greed Ain't Good

John Walsh

Bill Gates seems an unlikely candidate for sainthood. Google 'Bill Gates + evil' and you'll come up with 1.5 million matches. Among those results are conspiracy sites that have named him the Antichrist. It's a heavy label to lay on anyone, but Microsoft's ruthless pursuit of an information technology monopoly has clearly got a lot of people hot and bothered.

But tyrannical software czar is only Gates's day job — at least for the moment. In July 2008, Gates gave up his day-to-day responsibilities running Microsoft to concentrate on his charity work with the *Bill & Melinda Gates Foundation*.

Time management's a bitch for everyone. So how will Gates cope with taking over the world (part-time) and saving the world (full-time)? And why is the default voice of any article about Gates and his new role — including this one — so laced with irony? That's because we like our villains and heroes sharply drawn for easy recognition. Nelson Mandela: hero — easy. Saddam Hussein: villain — easy. So, why are a band of high-profile, New Age altruists muddying our nicely organised view of the world?

Within a month of Gates announcing his philanthropic intentions Warren Buffett — the world's *second* richest man (or *third* or *fourth* depending what day it is) — declared that he was giving eighty-five per cent of his stock, amounting to around $30 billion, to Gates's foundation.

So, when one of the world's richest men is giving the bulk of his fortune to an even richer guy, you know something significant is going on. Buffett's explanation was that he had always intended to give it away one day, and he felt the *Bill & Melinda Gates Foundation* could put it to better use than he could.

There has to be a problem with that somewhere. But in the meantime, what about that Oprah Winfrey? What a shameless self-promoter. Isn't being the Most Famous Woman in the World enough?

Now she's gone and built the *Oprah Winfrey Leadership Academy for Girls in South Africa*. The $20 million project aims to create a generation of empowered women in South African society by educating five thousand talented but underprivileged South African girls to realise their full potential.

Oprah's foundation is dedicated to the education and welfare of women, children and families in poor communities around the world. If you've only got about a hundred million or so to work with that's a well-targeted goal. But what does really big money buy you?

Gates hasn't just given up the role of Chief Software Architect at Microsoft to rattle a tin cup on the street corner. He has big plans and, with Buffett's help, is cashed up and ready to go. Gates's mission is to tackle the big three Third World diseases: malaria, HIV/AIDS and tuberculosis.

Malaria kills more African children than any other disease — around three million kids, most under the age of five, die each year.

The *Gates Foundation* was initially criticised for spending too much money on malaria research, so they recently stumped up

$35 million for nets, drugs and insecticides in Zambia that health authorities believe may cut deaths by seventy-five per cent within three years. Is there no end to this showboating and benevolent posturing?

What about that Angelina Jolie? Isn't it enough that she's the Sexiest Woman in the World? The *Maddox Jolie Pitt (MJP)* project seems to suggest not. The project has built the first Millennium Village outside Africa, linking ten disparate Cambodian villages and their six thousand villagers to create a sustainable community. Angelina and hubby Brad have built a soy milk factory and set up a plan to save the Cambodian elephant. She's visited thirty refugee camps in her role as a UNHCR Goodwill Ambassador and, well, if the last charitable thing you did was buy a box of Krispy Kreme donuts from the local girl guides, the whole thing makes you squirm with embarrassment.

But it seems that no good deed goes unpunished. The Gates-Buffett-Oprah-Angelina paradigm has a flipside: all of these famous philanthropists have been accused of attention-seeking. Paris Hilton turning up at a 'Save the Whales' rally in Venice Beach may be attention-seeking, but I'm not convinced that anyone giving away $30 billion is doing it to get attention. But even if attention is the prime motivation, does that diminish the value of the deed being performed? If three million African kids don't die of malaria next year does it really matter if Bill Gates gets his jollies writing the cheque?

Altruism is living and acting to help others. Philanthropy is the act of donating money, goods or time to help others. It doesn't say anywhere that these acts should be anonymous or shouldn't be performed by the rich and famous. I don't want to induce 'statistics fatigue' or 'list overload' but philanthropy is all about the numbers. So here's another one: in 2006, the richest people in the world donated about $285 billion to charities worldwide, many of them citing a 'moral obligation' to do so. Is 'moral obligation' code for 'guilt'? I don't know. Does the kid receiving a polio vaccination care? Probably not.

Both Gates and Buffett point to nineteenth century industrialist Andrew Carnegie as the inspiration for their philanthropy. As Buffett told *Forbes* magazine: 'We agreed with Andrew Carnegie, who said that huge fortunes that flow in large part from society should in large part be returned to society.' So maybe the African kid sleeping peacefully under the malaria-proof mosquito net should be squeezing another name into his nightly prayers.

Carnegie was *really, really, really* rich. In adjusted dollars he could have bought and sold Gates and Buffett combined. Carnegie's focus was public education. After retiring at sixty-five he dedicated his time to philanthropy, building three thousand public libraries across the US and Scotland. In all, he gave away around $380 million in old-school dollars (around $10 billion today).

A discussion of these case studies throws up all kinds of questions apart from motivation. What is the role of government in all this? The *Gates Foundation* currently provides seventeen per cent of the budget for the world's fight against polio. Why is the burden of activism and funding for basic human rights falling to a group of high-profile do-gooders? See Bono, Live Earth, Make Poverty History.

Factoring out the Gates-Buffett money, the top sixty donors in the US gave a median $60 million each to charities in 2006, compared with $33 million in 2005. These donors tend to be younger and mostly from the high-tech and high-finance sectors. And, because their donations tend to be results-driven, the power of each donated dollar is said to be greater than its equivalent in previous generations.

But do these humanitarian actions have a trickle-down effect? Is altruism on the rise among regular folk? Seven out of ten US charities raised more money last year than in 2005, and Australian charities reported a twenty-six per cent increase year on year.

But it isn't all about money. For the first time the Australian Census has measured volunteering.

The 2006 survey shows that around one in five Australians over the age of fifteen has engaged in voluntary work some time in their life. For the record, females were more likely to volunteer than males, Canberra was the 'volunteer capital' and Sydney had the lowest rate of volunteerism.

Sadly, altruism is a First World indulgence. If you were sweating it out for sixty cents an hour, sixty hours a week, making sneakers in a Manila factory you probably wouldn't be motivated to save the world on the weekend — even if you had one.

Another measure of altruism is attitude. The broad base of support across political lines for taking action to combat global warming seems to indicate a desire to do something that won't yield immediate gratification. Instead, it's a large-scale altruistic act purely for the benefit of future generations.

Maybe car pooling and taking shorter showers aren't on the same scale as unburdening yourself of $30 billion, but perhaps they are all part of an early twenty-first century realisation that Gordon Gekko got it wrong. Greed Ain't Good after all. Is it possible that this will be remembered as the Benevolent Century?

Will it be the Century that Saves the World? It seems cloyingly optimistic, but when the richest people in the world start giving their money away, the signs are almost biblical. If there is a pox on your family perhaps one of Bill's vaccines will be there to cure it.

Loving War

Cale Leslie Hubble

Prince Madric tentatively entered the old cottage — prepared for a fight, but not expecting one. Once inside he paused, drinking in the deluge of memories that came flooding back to him. Every scratch on the table, every knot in the wood-panelled walls, carried meaning to him. To him, and to someone else.

Comfortable now that there was no hired knife lurking in the single-roomed lodge, Prince Madric laid his sword down on the heavy, oak table. After a moment, he took off his regal headwear, his gloves and his jacket too — anything that could identify him with what he had become. In the weeks he spent here in his youth, he was simply Madric.

Madric spied an old mirror on one wall. Brushing the dust off, he was shocked to notice how weathered he looked now. He was not an old man, but the weight of the last few traumatic months seemed to have added years to his demeanour. Oh, for the lost innocence of youth, he thought, touching his thick beard and mangled brown hair. His wandering hands meandered their way to his crooked nose, and he was thrust back in time.

***

Madric was sitting atop another similar-aged youth, pummelling the boy's stomach with his fists, the victim's blonde hair flying. There was no malice, both adolescents were laughing uproariously.

'I think — I win — this time!' Madric said through bursts of laughter, his fists never still for a moment.

But the other boy's hand was edging its way towards a heavy stick nearby. 'I'm not — so sure!' he yelled triumphantly, swinging the branch in the direction of Madric's head.

The boy realised the mistake as soon as it connected with his friend. Madric fell backwards, clutching his bleeding nose, crying out in pain.

'What the hell!?' Madric screamed. The other boy leant over Madric, trying to find some way to help. But Madric's free hand had found the discarded branch — *crack* — his friend, too, collapsed to the ground.

They both lay on their backs, blood pouring from twisted nasal organs, and started laughing again...

***

Madric tore himself away from the mirror. Coming here had been a mistake. There were too many happy memories. Only memories.

With a stride, he was back at the table, reaching for his jacket. But before he had a chance to dress, he heard an all-too-familiar voice from the back door.

'Madric?'

He turned to face the newcomer. He knew him, of course, but could manage nothing more than a nod in recognition.

There was a pause.

'Looking well — ' the man began.

'Oh, cut the crap, Kyle. You've done enough of that already,' grunted Madric. He was eyeing his old friend down. Neat, straight, blonde hair, obscured by headgear rivalling Madric's in royalty. Clean-shaven, unerringly perfect. Iron-pressed military uniform, with the insignia strangely obscured.

Prince Kyle looked crestfallen. 'I thought I might find you here,' he said. When Madric was silent, he continued. 'I hoped I would.'

Madric made an incoherent noise. The pair remained in an awkward stand-off, looking into each other's eyes, the air electrified with the pressure of unspoken words.

'Sit,' muttered the bulkier Madric, and they both did. 'We need to talk.'

'Yes.'

Another pause.

'Do you remember the day I gave you your kingdom?' Madric asked.

***

'Of course I don't have a pass,' Kyle said to the guard, incredulous, 'I'm the best friend of the man of the hour — that gives me all the authority I need!'

The guard began a stern protest, but was cut off by a deep and gruff voice from within the chamber. 'Guard, let him proceed!'

The wide, carved oak doors were thrown aside, admitting the blonde, lean, smiling young man. 'You remember my voice,' he said.

Madric rose majestically from his throne and strode towards his friend, beaming. 'Wouldn't forget it in a million years,' he replied, as they embraced.

Kyle eyed the elaborately decorated room with awe. 'Congratulations are in order, it seems!'

'Monarchy must have been developed by simpletons. Least intellectually-demanding method of deciding upon a ruler I've ever discovered.'

'I'm sorry I couldn't make it to the funeral.'

'It's fine,' Prince Madric said, dismissing what seemed to be a painful topic. He was shuffling through some official-looking documents on his desk.

'You know I hold you in very high regard, Kyle.'

Kyle looked confused at this change of tone. 'And so you should!' he joked.

'I would trust you with my life, with everything I own,' Madric continued, ignoring his friend's attempts to distract him, 'and I hope you would do the same.'

Kyle nodded slowly.

Madric withdrew a single piece of parchment from his file. 'Then I have a proposal for you,' he said.

Kyle took the piece of paper suspiciously. Skipping to the bold font, his eyes seemed to pop out of his head. 'You're giving me half your kingdom?!'

Madric smiled. 'Not quite half,' he said. 'But close.'

Kyle's smile was still masked by shock. 'I — why — ' he said.

Madric placed his hands on the smaller man's shoulders. 'I know you've always dreamt about having your own kingdom, like you deserve. It's in your blood.

'Of course, there are conditions, like an indefinite alliance treaty, et cetera — but I can't imagine us fighting, can you? I won't make you sign anything. Brother kingdoms, eh?'

Kyle smiled despite himself. 'But what of the people? Surely they will dismiss this as brash and — '

'Never mind the people. They are fickle. They will grow used to the arrangement. You will be as good a ruler as I, Prince Kyle — probably better.'

Kyle's smile grew bigger until he was giggling, then laughing, cachinnating in disbelief and joy. The pair embraced once more...

***

'I remember it clearly,' said Kyle, revealing no emotion.

'You've — betrayed me, Kyle,' Madric struggled to speak the word that epitomised everything he was feeling. 'Betrayed.'

Kyle looked away, unable to withstand the intensity with which his old friend was looking at him.

Madric broke his stare too. 'When the first reports came in,' he began, his voice now trembling, his eyes welling with tears, 'I couldn't believe it. Villages near the border — attacked. Attacked. By whom? The troops of Prince Kyle.' Madric's voice cracked. He paused. 'You killed women and children, Kyle! How could you?!'

'It was not women and children,' Kyle murmured, eyes downcast.

'I don't care!' Madric said, standing and thumping his hands down on the table, taking that all-too-easy shift from tears to rage, yet still failing to draw in the other man's gaze. 'I trusted you, Kyle! All those years, all those memories.' He pointed at Kyle's nose. 'The greatest gesture there could ever be, Kyle, I gave it to you. And this is how you repay me? Invading my kingdom, murdering my men, what do you hope to achieve? Domination of the entire region? Crushing an old friend? *How could you?*' Madric repeated, breathing heavily.

Finally Kyle looked up at Madric. 'Recall the day we met,' he said, his voice as cold as steel.

***

The mighty King strode through the burning city with Madric, in his mid-teens, tagging along behind.

'And so the last city falls,' announced Madric's father. 'My kingdom is complete. Your kingdom is complete! This is a glorious day, son.' He ruffled the boy's hair.

But, try as he might, Madric could find no glory in the screams of a victim, a corner market consumed by flames, the whimpering of a stray dog down a lane. Madric spied a small figure, curled up into a tiny ball in an alleyway, trying to avoid the detection of the King's soldiers. Madric slipped away from his father and approached the other boy. 'What's your name?' Madric asked.

The figure lifted his tear-stained face. 'Prince Kyle,' he replied, without thinking.

'You're a prince?' said Madric eagerly. Kyle winced, shrunk into himself, cursing his lack of control. 'So am I!'

Now Kyle smiled.

'So what kingdom are you getting?' Madric continued excitedly.

'Umm,' Kyle hesitated, 'a foreign one. Over the mountains.'

'Oh.' Madric's eyebrows tensed up in consternation, 'Well why — ' But his inquiries were cut off by his father's booming voice.

'There you are! I was worried about you, son. Come on, we have revelling to attend to! Bring your little friend too, if you want.' The King had evidently indulged in pre-victory drinks.

Madric shrugged and looked at Kyle. 'Coming?'

***

'We never discussed again exactly *why* a foreign prince came to be hiding in the capital city of your enemy, did we?' Kyle continued.

Madric, still fuming, shook his head, the gesture magnified by his waving hair.

'I was not completely honest with you,' Kyle said in a monotone. Madric froze. Kyle continued. 'You should be aware that the kingdom your father obliterated that day — whose king was murdered by your father — is the same land you gave me to rule over. And I am heir to that kingdom.'

Madric's face fell. He felt his resolve melt away, and he collapsed back into the chair. 'I — God. Everything our — everything it was based on — everything I thought — were all lies?' he murmured. 'But still, why this, now?'

'My cabinet is made up of old patriots from my father's kingdom. They spread the word to the people of the lands you awarded me, whose allegiances still lie, deep down, with my father's throne, not yours.

'Word on the street was that the time had come to return the entire region to my kingdom's control — and I was the instrument to do so. By opposing their wishes, I was facing mutiny among my advisors, revolt among my people.'

There was an empty pause.

'I'm sorry,' Kyle finished lamely, his face portraying the truth of his words.

Madric looked desolate, despondent, desperate. 'Remember the times we spent here, together, in this very room?' Kyle did, but Madric continued anyway, as if trying to reinforce in his own mind everything they had shared. 'It was sometime before my father's death. I stole away from the castle, knocked on your window.'

'I was at the orphanage at that point,' Kyle added.

Madric nodded. 'We had no plans, no food. We were just two young lads with enough adrenaline to keep us alive for decades.'

'Remember our jubilation when we found this place?' They both smiled.

'We must have stayed here for a few months, at least.'

'It was only a matter of time till your dad found us, of course.'

'He sure had a habit of raining on our parade.'

They both looked up at each other. 'Good times,' they said together.

Madric lifted himself out of the chair, arms wide, beckoning.

Kyle removed his headdress, took a step forward, and joined his comrade in the embrace.

Kyle realised his mistake as soon as they made contact. Faintly, he heard the menacing sound of a flip-knife opening behind him.

Kyle crumpled to the floor. 'I'm sorry,' were the last words he heard.

Windows

Lyn Vellins

Warm light leaks like piss
around the edges of the windows
and trickles onto the dark earth
after it washes over
small trusting faces
over dirty dishes
and over love.

Outside, the night absorbs
the yellow light
sucks it into the half empty
bottle of whiskey beside me —

the ground underneath
me turns cold
as a stream of urine
lets go of its bodily warmth.

Picture

Raymond Baltas

picture a playground in a parish
a parish pictured through
the eyes of the innately sane
a painting without a frame
it seeps out, smearing
hues of the solitary, the birds
silhouetted by fiery reds... by blues

imagine
the bohemian infecting young children
with new and exciting prospects
with filthy ideas

picture pictures pictured
by people other than yourself

picture a place where
you're born in a correctional facility
because of original sin

picture being pictured as an
anachronism
picture the distasteful

think about snakes
wriggling like hands
down your pants;
how sinful, how dirty

picture the hands of the devil
idle in rest, yours trembling
with desire

take a picture of yourself
ejaculating on the cross,
on all fours while doing the rosary

because you shouldn't
because you can

take a picture of your neighbour's
dog humping your other neighbour's cat
leave it in their mailbox

picture all the iconoclasts of philosophy
past and present,
burning a church
building a playground
with the pages of manuscripts
to unbind young minds

take pictures of paintings and
burn them in a mass fire reminiscent
of Nuremberg 1933

paintings should be experienced
like magic mushrooms —
first hand

steal the pictures from
the Louvre, and replace them with
appropriations

take pictures of people sleeping
and picture them dead
using witty euphemisms
to describe the causes

live according to your inner
altar boy, and sin accordingly
even more so

die knowing you've pictured
the unpicturable, and know you'll
live on
through that which others may
now picture because of you

and lastly
picture your own death,
something ridiculous and
reflective of who you were —

a fucking nuisance,
who loved to dream.

The Delivery

Claire Marnane

At seventeen minutes past eleven o'clock, on Friday the twelfth of May, the doorbell rang in the Jones household. Sarah opened the door.

'Jonathon — it's arrived!'

Jonathon leapt out of the armchair where he had been half-dozing in front of the TV and hurried over to the front door where Sarah stood signing the delivery form. She handed the clipboard back to the burly delivery man with a tattoo of a large ungainly bird arcing across his bicep, and received, in exchange, a cardboard box.

Jonathon smiled nervously at the man. 'Nice bird,' he said, gesturing at the tattoo.

Ignoring him, the man checked the signature then turned and began walking back to his truck.

'Wait!' Jonathon yelped at him. 'Where are the instructions? We also ordered an instruction manual.'

The man continued inexorably on his way to the truck.

'Manual's in the box,' he threw back at them gruffly as he got in and started the engine.

'Well, I don't know what sort of service you call that!' Jonathon sputtered.

'Jonathon calm down, we have an instruction manual,' said Sarah.

'I still call that lousy service, leaving it with us and then driving off without even checking if it works or if we can understand the instruction manual or anything!'

She rubbed his shoulder reassuringly.

'Come on, we've been waiting a long time for this, let's go and open it and see if it's everything we hoped for.'

He smiled. Everything they hoped for. Yes, it was important to keep the big picture in mind.

They went into the lounge room to open the box. Jonathon used a sharp pair of scissors to cut the many layers of masking tape which had secured the box shut during its transit.

'Aahhh!' said Jonathon with a smile. 'It seems the bird man wasn't lying when he said the manual was in the box — hard to miss, actually!'

This last was in reference to the fluorescent, virulent green colour of the manual, apparently as an aid for harassed, multi-tasking people to find the book with ease.

Sarah peered into the box. It contained two more items, one small and narrow, and the other large and bulky. She removed the smaller package and unwrapped it.

'Ah. Remote control,' she said.

'Good! We'll need that!'

Sarah put the remote control down and turned back to the box.

'Here goes,' she said and lifted the bulky package from the box — very carefully, holding her breath.

She let it out on a sigh, smiling euphorically at him.

'Oh Jonathon, it's perfect! Really, so absolutely *perfect*!'

Jonathon nodded his agreement, gazing over at it, unable to wipe the smile from his face. 'It's a good shape, isn't it?'

'A perfect shape,' she said readily. 'And look at this good solid layer of bubble wrap they've attached to it. That's a really clever design feature, because it's likely to get knocked around when in use, but because it has this protective surface we won't have to worry about it getting damaged.'

Jonathon nodded happily. He opened the manual to page one and began reading aloud. It appeared to have been translated somewhat inexpertly from another language. 'Congratulation on you purchase of Ikokin product. We hope our product will meet all you expectation of high quality and reliability over many year of performance. All our product are designed specially with the purchaser to satisfaction. For any dissatisfaction with purchase, please call Ikokin customer service number on top of page.'

'That's good to know,' said Sarah, without ceasing her scrutiny of the product before her.

Jonathon nodded abstractedly. 'To begin the product use, first access of back to observe panelling in centre,' he read out, frowning. 'What the hell is that supposed to mean?'

'Hang on,' said Sarah, turning the product over to look at the back. 'I think I can see a different coloured panel here. Hand me those scissors. The manual must mean that we need to cut out a section of bubble wrap to access this panel on the back.'

She carefully cut out the bubble wrap on top of the coloured panel she could just discern through the layers of plastic, leaving a neat square hole in the wrapping.

'There! What does it say to do next?'

Jonathon consulted the manual. 'To activate product, press the large green button marked "Start".'

Sarah pressed the button and a faint whirring sound began emanating from deep within the layers of bubble wrap, pulsing gently, first louder, then softer. On the opposite side to the access panel, two orange lights blinked on and shone feebly, barely visible through the protective covering.

Sarah smiled. Everything they'd hoped for.

Soon they felt ready to move on to the next section of the instruction manual: How to Initiate Product Mobility.

The manual stated that, 'Mobility enablers (mobilisers) will need to manually extended when first use. Remove covering on base and extend mobilisers outwards. The ground interfaces at the tip of each mobiliser should be positioned at right angles to main functioning system.'

Sarah cut away the bubble wrap from this area, then removed a further plastic covering and pulled out two thin stick-like appendages contained within. Each had a hard knobbly ending with a flat surface on one side, which she pulled out at right angles from the product.

'Now, using remote controller or numeric buttons on access panel, enter code 3285732 and then press green "Start" button,' Jonathon read out.

Sarah entered the code and pressed 'Start'. The product whirred more loudly as the mobilisers began to move; the ground interfaces probed blindly for the carpet, then, finding it, the product righted itself so that it was standing up on the stick-like mobilisers.

Sarah clapped her hands delightedly. 'It's standing! All by itself!'

'Now, to make it walk, enter 7773826,' Jonathon read out.

The code was duly entered, and the product began to jerkily move itself around the room.

Sarah ran along in front of it taking photos of the unsteady steps.

'I've got to send these to Alison,' she said. 'She couldn't get hers to walk successfully this soon after arrival.'

'Well, she's not using the same manual as us,' Jonathon replied. 'What an idiot! There are some things in life you've got to take very seriously! What if she punches in the wrong buttons because she got a cheap, nasty manual? The thing might never start walking!'

Sarah shuddered in horror, imagining how awful it would be to have such a beautiful thing and then be negligent in programming it to function optimally. Then a horrible thought assaulted her... 'Jonathon, how would you know that your manual was faulty? I mean, Alison probably didn't realise there were better manuals out there and she probably thought she was doing the right thing all along... How would she know any better?'

Jonathon froze, struck by what she said. 'My god, you're right.' He thought for a moment. 'What we'll have to do is to look around at what other people's products are doing. That way we can gauge whether we're doing everything we should be doing with ours.'

So they began to go on outings with the product. They often saw other products on the way, in all sorts of different colours and shapes. Sarah was appalled at the callous way many makers had neglected to include protective covering on the different models. They began to feel reassured that they were doing everything right by their product, until one day... Jonathon saw it first and he stopped in his tracks, a shocked look on his face. Sarah's eyes followed his gaze; her hand flew to her face in horror — there, by the swings, was a man holding a large black circlet, and as she watched, his product leapt clean off the ground and sailed through to the other side of the circlet, landing neatly on its ground interfaces. Sarah looked down at her own product, which was no longer teetering so precariously on its mobilisers, but still retained a tendency to shuffle around aimlessly on its ground interfaces. Jonathon was riffling through the manual, searching for the chapter they must have missed.

'It's not here!' he hissed, frantic. 'There are no instructions for teaching it how to do that, nothing about jumping at all!' He took a deep breath to calm himself. 'Right.'

With that, he marched across to the man holding the circlet and saw, in the man's pocket, an instruction manual. It was not green like his own, but a rich red colour. So that was why. Instantly, Jonathon turned and headed for the shops to buy one for himself.

The red manual was found to have the added benefit of being written by a fluent anglophone. The chapter on Targeted Leaping with Your Product was towards the end of the manual.

'It must be quite advanced then,' Sarah commented.

'Good,' said Jonathon. 'We're up for this. Now, let's see what it says. "After activating the mobility function on your product, you may notice it has a tendency to mobilise itself even when you have not entered a mobilisation code. This is a normal function of this product, as it has been pre-programmed to move around its environment in certain ways to facilitate the achievement of training goals by the purchaser."'

He paused to nod appreciatively. It really was a much better manual than the last one. "The targeted leaping function is a great way to develop your skills as a trainer, and to get the most out of your product. The code to instigate leaping is 3420299; however, when initially training your product in this function, you will need to provide a stimulus on the opposite side of the target circlet to communicate your requirement that the product should leap in that specific direction. Small chocolates are a good choice of stimulus, as they combine an easy-to-identify colourful packaging with a high energy fuel to replace the energy lost in the act of repeated leaping, which may otherwise drain your product of power. Begin by positioning your circlet at ground height in front of your product. Position the chocolate on the other side, enter the program code above and press the green "Start" button. Repeat these instructions, gradually moving the circlet to higher positions from the ground as your product attains an acceptable success rate in the lower positions."

The targeted leaping function proved to be a challenging one. Sarah and Jonathon took turns training the product to meet their goals, but it was time consuming and laborious. The product tended to land badly on its ground interfaces, wobbling and stumbling into nearby objects.

'Thank god for the protective covering,' said Sarah fervently.

Yet although the covering had so far prevented any damage to the product throughout the training process, it was starting to show wear and tear of its own. Sarah frowned in consternation at the wide strip of bubble wrap that had unravelled at the top of the product. She'd already tried using sticky tape to secure it in place to no avail. Now she took her staple gun from the drawer in the study and sat down next to the product. Holding the bubble wrap taut across the top of the product, she used the staple gun to fix the bubble wrap onto it. The tiny metal shards rasped against the sides of the product as they clawed the plastic securely in place millimetres from where the faint flickering of the two orange lights shone faintly through.

'There,' she said, 'now nothing can hurt you.'

Soon Sarah was pleased enough with her work with the product that she called her friend Alison to talk about it.

'It's been four weeks now and we're so proud of what we've achieved. It leaps through the circlet with only intermittent chocolate bars now; mostly we only need to enter the code!' she gushed.

'How fantastic!' Alison gushed back. 'Ours reached that stage of training after only two weeks, but it *is* a different product, so it's probably a bit silly to compare them like that.'

Sarah felt a pang of irritation.

'Well, it really is going awfully well,' she said. 'It's a pity nobody else can appreciate how much work you put into these things, and how much skill it takes to achieve these outcomes.'

'Is your product involved in any competitive targeted leaping?' Alison asked casually. 'We've entered ours in one; it's only a bit of fun of course, but... '

The targeted leaping competition took place in an auditorium filled with tense, edgy people, fussing over their products, grimly applauding the competition. There were other competitions taking place in smaller, cordoned-off sections of the auditorium, far away; over here were products shuffling around in various patterns making tapping noises, and elsewhere, products emitting rhythmic vocal functions. But they were small competitions, obviously unimportant. Jonathon gazed around him. These were the people he wanted to impress, their products of the finest quality and impeccably trained. Many well-dressed people held shining circlets of silver and gold. Sarah and Jonathon watched and clapped politely as a stream of products surged relentlessly through the competition, gliding effortlessly through their trainers' circlets and landing with precision.

Soon, Jonathon was the next to display his product. He fidgeted with the remote control in his sweaty hands. He had memorised the leaping code weeks ago, but recently he had also memorised the 'power' code, or 'how to release an additional burst of power to the main functioning system in the event of an emergency'. He looked up as polite applause filled the auditorium and the product ahead of them mobilised itself off the stage after its trainer. Jonathon moved onto the stage; the product trailed on behind him. Jonathon entered the 'bow' code and pressed 'Start'. They bowed in unison. They took their places. Jonathon took a deep breath and entered the two required codes, followed by the green 'Start' button. The product whirred violently, then bounded powerfully up off the stage and soared through the circlet in Jonathon's outstretched hand. From the sidelines, Sarah's eyes filled with tears of pride. But then there was a gasp from the people around her. They had seen that the product was moving too fast, and was altogether at the wrong angle to land properly. As in a nightmare, Jonathon watched as the product crashed awkwardly to the ground; shrieks of horror filled the air as its mobilisers snapped under its weight, and the blinking orange lights were smashed against the floor.

At the air-conditioned, tastefully decorated customer service offices of Ikokin Pty Ltd, a pleasantly smiling woman walked over to greet Sarah and Jonathon, who sat seething with an awful combination of humiliation, anger, distress and regret.

'I understand that you've had a problem with your product, specifically with the targeted leaping function,' she said to them, before transferring her gaze down to the product.

She paused, taking in the bubble wrap stapled onto it, the jagged ends of the broken mobilisers feebly mended with sticky-tape. Her eyebrows rose a fraction.

'Are you aware that the packaging hasn't been removed from this product?'

Sarah and Jonathon looked at each other in surprise.

Sarah answered, 'We thought it was supposed to be like that.'

'Covered in bubble wrap?' came the slightly dubious reply from the customer service representative. 'Well, I suppose you wouldn't be the first to think that. Normally it's not a problem for our consumers, but in this instance it's unfortunately prevented you from noticing that this isn't actually a targeted leaping model.'

Sarah and Jonathon gasped, horrified.

The woman continued on smoothly, 'According to our records, your product is a rhythmic movement model — that's the primary function it was designed for and it's been pre-programmed to excel in training focussing on this function. Perhaps you noticed a tendency for it to shuffle around when not responding to your coding?' she prompted gently.

But they hadn't even heard her; they were staring down at the product beside them, suddenly a usurper, a worthless broken thing crumbling all their dreams and hard work. Angry disappointment flooded over them.

The customer service representative continued on more brightly. 'The good news is, as the damage has occurred within the six-month warranty period you are entitled to a replacement model.'

'Oh no,' said Jonathon, shocked, 'we couldn't do that.'

'We're far too fond of it,' Sarah agreed.

Moth

Amelia Walkley

like fighter pilots, zooming jets
lying in wait, wings fanned, spanning and resting
then, from their apparent dormant slumber
they rise, flitting, answering the light's temptress call
powdersoft, those wings
yet strangely repulsive — in their erratic vibration
that funny brown dust, a residue
    I would rather not have to wipe away

this conference of moths is most unwelcome

Two Ways

Cathleen Inkpin

Two ships pass in the night. Two ships pass into moonlight and fade. In the morning there are only shadows on the water, washed away with the tide.

***

Annie grows up in the suburbs: four-bedroom, 2.4 kids and a lawn with sprinklers. It is half an hour to the city, a quarter to the motorway, ten minutes from the train line and less than an inch from neighbourhood gossip. On weekends she plays with freckled George from no. 14, and rides her bike with sometimes-bossy Emma from no. 26. Their 0.4, Howie the Jack Russel, stays nights with Mrs Mackenzie and her poodle.

In the late afternoon, Annie likes to sit in the tree at the end of the street and draw the returning traffic, regular like clockwork.

Her father is a solicitor, her mother a dentist, her brother a pain (almost always) and they all have blonde hair, except Annie.

***

Ellen passes quietly into moonlight at eighty-nine. She dies as she lived, alone with few friends save a coffee shop owner, a couple of long-lapsed eccentrics and her next-door neighbour. She is tidy in death, all that remains: a comic book and a photograph of a girl, wide-eyed and young, riding a bicycle over the crest of a hill in the middle of the city.

***

On the first day of Year 7, Annie plaits her hair on the right side and somehow winds up popular. Netball captain and photographer for the school magazine, her life is always busy. So busy she sometimes loses herself to it.

She always feels at the edge of life, barefoot at a precipice, eyeing the ocean but too scared to dive in. Only the camera helps with that. She can zoom and focus in on things, gain glimpses of herself and glimpses of the world that others don't or can't see because they are distracted. Angles and light, expressions of glee and flickers of distress are all exposed in fractions of a second. Fleeting flashes of a world Annie is at once one with and shuttered from. One frame clicks over to the next.

***

Slipping into the obscurity of old age, Ellen is able to spend hours observing the world from a distance, undisturbed. It is a shot of the unexpected, therefore, when it stares right back.

Ellen thinks she might be being followed when the man she'd been painting on the harbour-side park bench doesn't move for the four hot hours of midday sunlight. She thinks he must know what she's up to and desire, by some narcissistic purpose, to see the finished product. It's fair enough really, but she's always hated presumptuous people. She packs up and starts walking home.

That's when she *knows* she's being followed, and when she turns, easel swinging to her side with a dangerous jerk, he knows that she knows. He is tall, perhaps five years her junior with faded blonde hair, silver at the edges, and his eyes on hers are strangely intimate, as though he recognises her somehow when Ellen knows him only as a stranger.

She waits, but he just ducks his head, runs a nervous hand through silver strands and shrugs carelessly when he says, halting, that he's an admirer of her paintings, that she reminds him of his sister — who died recently, and could... maybe would she like to see some of her work? His eyes, half sheepish, half beseeching are laden with a sheen of grief that catches sharp on the late afternoon sunlight. She shrugs reluctantly, says she has the time.

It is the photographer whose pictures were in the coffee shop and she can hardly catch a breath for a moment when she sees it laid out there. Hundreds of prints, pinned and hung, framed and scattered on the floor, dusty and glistening good as new, marking a life lived through a lens. It is the half of life Ellen had caught only moments of, the half that had always escaped her imagination, and there, amongst it all, a moment that is purely her own, shared now (she realises) with another.

***

College is a mess of ambitions and confusion, of missed opportunities.

Annie meets Greg waiting in the coffee line the second day on campus. He is George from no. 14's brother, three years older and instantly funny, with an uncanny ability to read her mind. He's an architecture major and they discuss corners and curves, how to draw the perfect circle. He is everything she is used to, her best friend, the boy next door, and it is the most dangerous thing in the world.

'It's just me,' he tells her, 'trust me.'

She misses the chance for an apprenticeship, a trip overseas, so they can spend time with his family, the one she saw every weekend on their veranda, washing their car, pinning out the laundry. It's so simple to settle back into him and this, spend lazy afternoons taking pictures of his flowerbeds and not thinking about the future.

They move out together, get engaged and she is pregnant and married in a sudden turn of the tide, her dreams shelved with the tupperware while they set up home.

***

After ten years, he can't take the noise and awkwardness of the city any longer, his feet have started to itch, and hers stopped long ago. Ellen will never leave the city now, she knows, it's engraved on her soul somehow. They part amicably, only a bit of fuss, because they are both used to being alone, putting themselves first. Perhaps that is her one true sin in life.

One day she sends the comic, finished at last, to a publisher and it is issued in a limited release. Two girls stare up at her from the pages: one flying high in the clouds, on her way to a great adventure, the other sitting at the breakfast table with her family, yawning over cornflakes, pretending to the world that her life is ordinary. She wonders who will be thought of first.

***

Back in the suburbs again, domestic life begins to grate on Annie sooner than she expected. Tess, though, is a beautiful child, creative and enthusiastic, and Annie's favourite hour is 6 pm when Greg comes home and tells them all long fairytales about his day, beautiful lies that lull them into contented sleep.

Once Tess is away to school, Annie breaks out the camera and takes to the streets. She likes café scenes, the busy chatter of lives explained over lattes and the steady push of feet and cars going by. That's where she sees the girl, wild and free, flying over the top of the hill like something possessed, lit up and shining like a promise, a beacon on the horizon. That is me, she thinks.

***

Ellen doesn't marry him, but they settle in together and she paints murals on his café walls. His friends and her neighbour laugh over their 'mutual midlife crush' and say they act like a couple of teenagers. He says she reminds him of an artist he's fond of — points to a couple of landscape photographs of the coast behind the coffee-maker, and one hanging beside the oven in the kitchen: a city shot of restless, gossiping, young faces under umbrellas on a sidewalk café. It looks like so much of her youth, and she chokes on a few laughing tears. It's not that she's unhappy to be old, she has no regrets, no missed opportunities to be bitter about; she just isn't sure how to handle contentment.

***

Tess is old enough now to remind Annie of her long-latent, youthful ambitions and make the hunger for them resurge. She gets a job taking school photos and wants to rip her hair out... wants to give sagely advice to the kids whose personalities and aspirations she can see through the lens cap.

Greg is spending more time at the office and more time with his female co-worker, and Annie's deep-seated anxiety — that stability and normality can never be satisfactory — emerges again.

Then one day she sits down and writes a letter to a magazine pitching a family road trip across the desert, grabs Greg and Tess and sets off, not telling them that she has yet to receive a reply. Greg thinks it's a quarter-life crisis, but the time is good for them, and the photos get picked up. She begins to freelance pictures. The desert and the road make landscape more interesting to her; the universal isolation and vitality are both appealing to her. When she becomes pregnant again she makes a series of self-portraits, careless and confident enough now to make them truthful, and a gallery is interested.

***

Ellen finds love late in life: a coffee shop owner with a wicked smile who always puts an extra sugar in her latte. He holds her hand through her father's funeral and takes her to the zoo two weeks later. She enjoys it for the first time, no longer alone.

***

They move out of the city and up the coast. It is fresh air and space and Annie feels for the first time that she's living a life she's chosen for herself.

***

Ellen comes home because her visa expires, because she has to. She had been dreaming of living in Mexico, Southern California or maybe Texas... somewhere with desert or a coastline to whisk her thoughts out to sea. Of course home has both of those, so she returns, slips into her forties, takes a teaching diploma and ends up in a community college teaching pottery and fine art, and drawing comics for kids in her spare time that maybe one day she'll send to a publisher, though her ambition has started to wane with her age.

Her parents visit often, because she's finally bought a house in the suburbs and they think she's decided on a normal life after all. They bring house gifts — a food processor and bottles of wine — and bad news.

Ellen ends up watching her mother slowly lose her beauty, passing into whiteness and nothing when cancer ends up in her brain. Her father, retired long ago, asks to move in and she allows it. She sells their apartment and puts the money away for a rainy day.

She's become far too practical, she thinks some days, too conventional... but there's no artistic crowd to jeer at her any longer for it. She makes friends with the woman next door and shares cooking recipes and red wine, and babysits her kids. She still dreams of the sea, can smell and see herself there, but rarely leaves town.

***

Life ticks on and Annie's photography mellows. There are more landscapes, particularly of the coast, and she starts dreaming of another self, still alone and wandering. Her parents both pass away in the space of a few months and she thinks about tracing her real heritage, talks about it with her brother, wonders why she wants to find out now, when she is almost at peace with herself, rather than before when it was such a struggle. In the end the idea passes with the tide.

***

Ellen is getting older. She can feel it in her bones somehow, in her itchy feet and itchy fingers that long to wander and sketch/draw/paint new things before they become weary and ordinary like herself. She leaves her friends, who have all begun to realise their age too and started to pair off, settle down, look for houses, jobs, careers, legitimacy and security.

She travels alone overseas, up through Asia and Russia, in the winter so the air will paint her arms in pinpricks of pain and make the beating of her heart loud and precious. She makes it to Italy by spring, laughing like a child over the gondolas and the marble cathedrals, the sacred and the profane, the hot cheese of the pizza that stings as it burns hot on her tongue. She laughs like a child because she can feel it slipping away with every footprint she makes on the earth.

She bypasses Britain (too familiar), gets trashed in Canada, and only starts to remember again when she stops the hire car at the Grand Canyon. She shouts her name and it comes back twice. It is bigger than her imagination could conceive, too big to draw, too majestic to try to draw, to capture from real sight. It steals her breath till she's heaving over the side, long, wracking sobs that tell her she's finally connected with something, though *what* she's not sure she'll ever know.

***

Greg dies.

One day he's sitting on the porch and just stops breathing. Heart attack, the doctors say, common, apparently. She decides to move back into the city, now Tessa is gone and the house feels big and empty, with a draught and a chill in the evenings she never noticed before.

She strolls the city streets and passes that hill where she saw the wild girl one day, looks in the mirror and can't see a trace of it. The dreams return, and this time maybe it's the other her who's happily coupled and she is the lonely wanderer.

***

Ellen does go to college for a time, mostly absent for a couple of semesters. She draws cartoons, has started one of those superhero comics about a normal girl with a secret identity.

She's got it all spread out in a cafe one day, one of those hip, off-the-city-drag, hippy places with upside down milk crates for seats, and the waiter takes a liking to it, to her, pins it up on the noticeboard and says he's got a friend who publishes indie, amateur stuff he can get to take a look at it. So she falls in with the artistic set, and the phone calls home become less frequent.

She's moved out of the apartment and into a little cottage with a few drama kids, they're messy but she's used to that — it's what her headspace supplied when her home was so neat, so rich, so sterile. She buys a bike and rides it like she's on fire, drops out of college and takes a paper route, works in a friend's gallery and continues writing the comic about the girl, from the small town, with wings.

***

Annie travels abroad for the first time, with a friend from high school who long ago moved back to the old country. She treads cobbled streets and huge history museums and thinks that it's only when you are old that you realise you are about to become part of it — something that's been and trodden on and passed away, leaving only bits and pieces of itself behind.

Her younger self would have only been thrilled by what's here now, to be a living thing beside it, walking miles every day and drawing sketches in her mind at a thousand strokes a minute — for later when she got too weary to see it all properly. That self would have left the travelling for the young ones, thinking it too bittersweet and tiresome, and only for those who didn't take the opportunity when first offered. She thinks she can see that younger self, a vivid thing, flaunting her little French and laughing as though she could never quite stop.

***

Ellen attends an all-girls Catholic high school and her parents are overprotective without saying why. They keep telling her how special she is to them, how they thought they'd never have her.

She runs away for one day. She takes the car, which her parents bought her for her final year of school, and flies up the coast, roof down, with a scarf to catch the wind, feeling young, free and reckless. She savours the salt that whips her cheeks and shouts joy to the world, though she is far from joyful. She has no real friends and a weird sense that she is out of her body half the time, floating around searching for something. People say she's an eccentric and that she should go to art school.

***

Annie dies as Greg did, quiet, almost on a sigh. A normal, comfortable, common way, like her life. Had she known she'd have wished a little eccentricity to it, wished to die on a beach on some island exotic. But she died in contentment, her daughter by her side, the 'might have beens' and the 'if only's' whispered away with the closing of her eyes.

***

Ellen grows up the only daughter of two investment bankers, living in a high-rise with a nanny and a view. Left alone with only her imagination for company, occasional visits to the fun park or the zoo, Spanish classes and karate, she is a strange and introverted child with a strange and inward-turned childhood. She is intelligent and artistic, creating whole worlds of creatures and people to entertain herself. Her favourite toy is a doll her father brought back from Switzerland that looks just like her — brown hair with a slight wave and a mouth that turns up on the left side. She and the doll, Alice, have all kinds of adventures together... if only she were real.

***

Two heads lie side by side on a hospital bed. Cast off and soon to be separated, two sets of twin eyes, brown and blinking look into each other and see themselves. Two lives diverge, meet and pass away. Two ways, led by two hearts, start and end never knowing that the other existed.

My Dearest, Darling Beatrix...

Amelia Walkley

My dearest, darling Beatrix,

Yes, I am aware that this is a, shall we say, rather unconventional material on which to be writing to you. I beg you, please, do not be any more disgusted with me than you already are. I swear to you, my dear, that this is the only paper I have left in the house.

You see, I've been on a bit of a stream of consciousness frenzy of late, and as a result I've already finished up that ream of Reflex that I pinched from work, as well as all of your floral-edged writing paper. (You know, with the forget-me-nots.) Gone (or rather, scripted) is an entire roll of brown paper, the last of it I'm afraid, so you'll need to remember to pick some more up next time you go to Woolworths, not to mention all of my blank postcards, notebooks and envelopes, and even the backs of every cereal box I managed to scrounge from the recycling bin. I considered taking my pen to the walls but then thought better of it. After all, we did just have a new coat applied with the recent renovations and all, though I never was partial to that duck shell blue which you so adored. But I digress. The fact remains that there is nothing but this left, my dear, and I have stooped to this level because I feel it important that you are made aware of what I've been going through.

You must understand, sweet, my irrevocable obligation to preserve every single thought, musing, contemplation and deliberation which should cross my mind. Pure white swans, so elegant, feathered and sculpted, reel down the river of the psyche, anthropomorphic projections of every and any of my notions, then, taking flight, they soar into the depths of blissful oblivion... Oh, so wretched am I! I cannot even be spared a minute of the egression of my intellectual piffle to adequately explain my situation. I apologise profusely, my dear, for that most unwelcome intrusion of entirely unnecessary prose.

You see, after your spontaneous departure the other day, I so foolishly indulged in prolonged and intense sessions of navel-gazing. Consequentially, I just cannot seem to switch off my mind, nor halt my hand once it is with pen. It is an impulse which has become more than slightly problematic: in fact I should say it has reached an almost critical stage.

I should very much like it if you were to recommend to me a specialist in the area of obsessive-compulsive stream of consciousness authorship. I thought you, being in the publishing industry and all, might know of a good one. Who did that Kerouac fellow go to, anyhow? My condition really is becoming quite unbearable. Not only do I find myself with no spare time to prepare myself any form of victuals with which to sustain my body in its production of a constant stream of self–induced prose, I haven't even slept a wink this past week, not since I took that pen to hand and started on the crisp, blank sheets of A4. This letter to you is a respite of sorts, but still involves pen and paper and the imprinting of thoughts on a page. May God help me.

I've reached further inside myself and drawn up all manner of dark past secrets this last week. At times it was almost meditative, trance-like, all the while frantic. You should see the red marks on my hand, in the fork 'twixt finger and thumb where rests my pen! And the glorious ink stains, like blossoming bruises, pricey pockmarks — evidence of this Author's Curse. I'm not sure if I'll ever be able to get them out, no matter how much Pears soap and hot running water I should apply. Anyway, there's no time for hand washing. It's a wonder I've even made it to the bathroom. It was the last place left, though, from which to source my unusual and relentless demand for paper.

If ever this missive finds its way to you, Beatrix dear, I should think it would be time to call the hospital. It could almost be too late, as I'm not sure I'll be able to break the spell for long enough to get to the post office, and even if I did somehow make it there, I'm sure they'd not allow me to post this. It wouldn't all fit in a normal envelope for a start, and I've no doubt I'd be on the receiving end of many a perplexed stare.

If you ever do come home, you'll find the house in such a state — you see, there wasn't time to devise a logical system of filing for my personal note taking, and it's got to the stage where everything's strewn about the place a bit. Currently I'm entwined in metres and metres of toilet roll (it will keep unravelling once I've written the words), which is another reason to doubt that this letter will ever get to you in time.

What's this? Do the letters seem to become more and more faint as I write? My pen is running low on ink, see how it fails, my words are fading. Also, it's not the best surface to be writing on, I must admit. A little too soft, and I'm sure that perfume affects the ink somehow. Oceanic Breeze, and why they feel the need to scent the stuff is beyond me. This is it, darling Beatrix. I'm afraid once the pen runs dry I'm not exactly sure what's going to happen. I can't really stand up for all this toilet tissue, which is in the process of mummifying me slowly (though I assure you, I feel no pain), and I'm scared that if ever I stop this stream of consciousness caper, the results upon my state of mind are sure to be severely catastrophic. There it goes... the last of it, not even a blot left in it. I...

Tangled

Rachel Barratt

A ring of extra-strong paracetamols decorates the desk. Clancy takes a sip of water to ease the tablets down her throat. It is the first time she has swallowed three at once. Her fists pummel against her head. A sealed envelope contains a letter to her mother. Clancy places the rest of the tablets in her palm. 'It would be so easy to take them all,' she murmurs.

The paracetamols brush against her unglossed lips. She is interrupted from the final act by a sharp knocking resonating against the bedroom door.

'That boy is outside waiting for you again, revving up his blasted engine,' her mother says wearily.

She scatters the paracetamols into her purse as she tells herself that it will have to wait. Clancy pulls a shapeless, striped cotton dress over her sagging underwear. She frantically searches for the cardigan, which still carries a hint of her sister's scent. Bracelets adorn Clancy's wrists and cover the tiny scars.

Joel blows smoke rings in the air. A trilby hat perches on the top of his head. From an open window he recites the lyrics, which are scrawled in eyeliner pencil on the back of a shopping receipt. Clancy only climbs into the car after he dangles a half empty bottle of vodka in front of her. Lifting it to her mouth, she is numb to the feelings of his kisses on her neck. He looks ahead and drives, whilst Clancy dangles her arms out of the window and presses her feet against the dashboard.

'Thank you,' she mumbles as they arrive at the location for her Saturday job.

Inside the art college, a man with greying sideburns and a thin goatee offers her a robe. She undresses in a make-shift cubicle with curtains that do not quite reach the ground. Her purse is temporarily placed away in the locker. The class of students enters, and she makes her way to the small stage in the center of the room, which is built from wooden blocks. Clancy unties her robe and exposes her pale, small breasts. Silvery stretch marks faintly trace the outline of her hips. She smiles internally at the predictable reaction of a new undergraduate class; the nervous glances, the unblinking stares, the stifled laughs and the one student who starts sketching manically. Clancy revels in being the focus of their attention. She is always aware of the irony; during school plays she always watched from the side curtain, as girls resembling cover models performed the lead roles. Here Clancy could act out all the possibilities of being someone else. Some days she would cake her face with white foundation and spider her eyes with lashings of black eye shadow and mascara; whilst other times she would drape her sister's designer jewelry around her neck.

She looks at their sketches during the short coffee break. Sometimes, she hardly recognizes herself in the metamorphoses of images they create of her with enlarged breasts and bee-stung lips. Today, there is only one picture that captures her roving eye. The artist has etched the outline of a waif-like girl drowning in her own tears;

Clancy traces her finger around the outline. She moves towards the locker and fumbles with the combination lock. Her heart palpitates. She reaches out towards the purse, but she hears the idle chatter of the returning students winding its way up the corridor, and reluctantly decides to leave it there for now.

Clancy remembers how her friends used to tell her to enroll in an art course. They were completely unable to understand the effort that went into retaining a certain pose for two hours at a time. Clancy used to like revealing her part-time profession as a life model at her mother's lame tea and scone parties. Choisin had died four months ago. Now her mother would still be lounging in her nightdress during the afternoons, as she talked to herself. Choisin's death changed everything.

After the students have packed away their art supplies, Clancy strolls over to the studio where Joel is rehearsing. The band members nod their heads in acknowledgment before the drummer starts to play, bringing in the beat. The floor is strewn with pizza boxes and a pyramid of beer bottles. Clancy swigs from the almost finished vodka bottle in an attempt to block out her whirling thoughts of whether to slip the tablets onto her tongue. She opens an old shoebox, which is crammed with Joel's photographs. Some of them are stuck together and pictures of Joel's grandma's wedding day are interspersed randomly with recent pictures of Clancy.

Clancy remembers his darkroom, where photographs hung off the washing line like wrinkled shirts. Faces would emerge that Clancy did not recognise; an old lady rinsing her clothes in a walnut brown

Indian river, or the profile angle of a blind busker with his fingers hovering over a saxophone. Clancy used to spend hours rearranging the pictures, jotting down the different stories which sprouted from her imagination. Rejection letters from various magazines had been burned with the flame of her cigarette lighter. Her purple notebooks remain abandoned ever since the day her mother allowed the life support machine to be switched off.

None of the photographs of Clancy are posed. A black and white image of Clancy laughing with her sister appears in the pile. Clancy fingers the lock of Choisin's bone-straight hair, which she keeps in her bag. She saved it at the start of her illness, when Choisin shaved her head. Clancy had wanted to collect things that she would be able to touch later, so she would never forget her sister. Choisin had refused to talk about the inevitability of her death. Even in the womb, Clancy had always been the strongest one physically, weighing nine pounds, whilst a two pound Choisin lay in an incubator, with Frankenstein-like wires attached to her body. Their mother had stared over the incubator for hours, leaving her healthy child to scream like a vulture for milk. The relief emanating from the family when Choisin was finally released from hospital was overwhelming. None of them could have guessed that sixteen years later this hospital would become more familiar to them than their own home.

Clancy had been angry with Choisin after the first diagnosis of leukaemia. Choisin had been her only friend at school. Afterwards Clancy remembered that, being forced by the teachers to go to the lunch hall. The only days that were bearable were when she managed to sneak a corner place with the older kids on a table. Sometimes Clancy had sat alone on the long bench, pretending not to notice the other pupil's stares which she could almost feel imprinted on the back of her shirt. She was the weird twin. Her sister on the other hand, always had at least two year groups trying to ingratiate themselves with her, hoping for a spot on her party invitation list.

Choisin did not look that ill initially as she remained at home to watch daytime television and eat spoonfuls of ice-cream whilst the other twin was left to struggle with her science exams. Clancy stopped ignoring her when Choisin's hair started to fall out in clumps overnight. Gifts of hideously patterned silk scarves from their mother's friends remained buried in a drawer. Clancy would climb into her bed at night, when the sobbing started. She squeezed her sister's hand softly and stayed awake until Choisin fell asleep.

In an attempt to distract herself from these raw fragments of memory, Clancy closes the box and looks ahead through the glass screen of the studio. She notices the girl grasping the microphone stand with her lacquered pink fingernails. She straightens her tight grey pinafore dress before she adds the husky backing vocals. Joel does not look at her but Clancy knows. It was the first month after Choisin died. Joel's sweaty hands had clamored over Clancy's skin, while his body begged for sex. Clancy pushed him aside. Joel had asked how long it would take for their relationship to go back to normal, but no words escaped from her tight throat. Not long after he had auditioned the new female singer for their band, he stopped pleading for sex. At first Clancy told herself that she did not mind; all she wanted was to lie in Choisin's bed. It was here where Clancy's hands possessed control over the razor blade, which refreshed almost healed cuts on her wrists. The vermillion blood that always bubbled to the surface offered Clancy a sensation of inexplicable calm.

Joel announces to Clancy through the intercom system that their final version of their latest song has just been recorded. For the first time Clancy does not wait to hear the new tune. She rushes to stand in the toilet cubicle, where she stares at the tablets in her hand. The bathroom door creaks as it opens and the sound of heavy boots thud against the tiles.

'Clancy, are you okay?' Joel asks.

No, and I haven't been for three whole months, Clancy considers saying, but instead replies curtly, 'I'll be right out.'

Joel sighs and lights another cigarette. Their relationship used to be so easy, days spent on the cliff tops overlooking the sea, interspersing their time between writing and making love. Now, when he looks at her, there is a far-away look in her eyes, she is physically present but it is as if her mind is in a foreign land, where he is incapable of speaking the language. His fingers drum on his leg before he leaves the bathroom.

She watches all the tablets dance away in circles, after one short flush. Clancy visualizes herself stepping off the cliff tops and sacrificing her body to the endless ocean. Graffiti on the toilet door flutters her mind back to the night of the junior school prom. Clancy had never wanted to go; but it was as if Choisin was holding onto life just to make it to this momentous occasion of adolescence. A blue silk dress had been displayed above her bed for the last three months. She refused help as she stood up weakly from her wheelchair. The material now swamped her shrinking frame. Her reflection in the mirror flashed back a platinum blonde wig that emphasized her pallid skin that had missed the sun of the last two summers. When the doorbell chimed, Choisin had announced that she could not go to the prom. Clancy offered to stay, but her sister begged her to go. When Clancy returned in the early hours of the morning, Choisin was able to live out the minute details of her only prom through her sister's eyes. Clancy had even danced with her twin's childhood sweetheart and intended date, the school's soccer captain, Jake Denning.

Clancy drifts out of the day dream and she rifles through the studio closet. Joel's leather jacket has fallen to the floor. Clancy retrieves his car keys and slips out of the studio. The sun glints through the ghost blue clouds. She is unaware of the drivers beeping their horns to alert her of the need to switch on the headlights in the fading light. The acceleration increases with firm taps of her foot on the pedal.

She spies a glimpse of the silhouette of a tall man standing beside the road. As Clancy approaches, she slows the car as she debates whether or not to offer him a lift. Thick straps of a rucksack dig into his shoulders. Clancy gingerly winds down the window handle.

'Hi,' he says. 'Are you going as far as Myrtle point?'

'Almost, just before there,' she lies, not wanting any more interruptions to her plan.

Without waiting for an invitation, he simply climbs into the car. Clancy stares at his trainers, which are gaping with holes. She continues to drive. Please don't let him be one of those incessant talkers, she prays, turning up the volume of the radio.

The man inspects his sunburned forehead in the mirror, before he ties back his long unbrushed hair. He struggles to remove a thick winter coat. Clancy recoils for an instant as she detects the stale odour which now pervades the car. She notices that his hands fidget nervously over the opening of the rucksack.

'You're nearly out of petrol.' He offers his first words after a half hour of driving.

'Damn it.' Clancy glances down at the orange light. She had no idea when it started to flash. It is another fifteen miles to the next petrol station. Clancy considers the possibility that she might have to walk to Myrtle Point, although that would involve her hitchhiker joining her.

The engine splutters as she parks outside the petrol station. Clancy rifles through Joel's wallet finding only a few coins and scraps of lyrics. Her passenger offers no money. She counts out five dollars in change and hopes that will suffice. Clancy tugs at the petrol cap and she lightly presses the pump's trigger. But the digits reach nine dollars before she has the chance to stop the flow of liquid.

'I'm four dollars short.' Her eyes plead to the hitchhiker.

He shrugs his shoulders and looks back blankly.

'Great!' Clancy's credit card has already reached the limit.

Clancy waits to talk to the younger attendant. She lowers the neckline of her dress and perfects her girl in distress voice, 'I couldn't stop the pump at five dollars, it kept going.'

'That's not my problem. Nine dollars please, Miss.'

'But I only have five.'

'Nine dollars, Miss.'

'Here's five.'

'Look, kid, you're going to have to call your mother.' He hands her the telephone receiver.

She visualizes her mum having to leave home, climb into the car and drive to the station shivering, still dressed only in her cotton night dress. A beeping sound rings throughout the shop as a policeman enters through the door. He peruses the row of dripping hot dogs turning in the microwave oven. Clancy's hands start to feel clammy as she thinks about the driving test she failed last month.

Back in the car, the man slowly fingers the zips of his bag. Finally he opens the top compartment, which reveals the glimmer of a silver knife blade. He debates over using it now or saving it for later.

'I think my friend has the cash. I'll be right back,' Clancy announces.

The policeman and attendant are staring at Clancy through the glass as they talk about her. Clancy notices in the wing mirror that the man sitting in the passenger seat is gripping a knife. He reaches into another section of his bag and fumbles to find an object. Clancy looks back and forth between the policeman and the hitchhiker, unsure of where to turn.

The stranger reveals an apple and starts to unpeel the skin of the fruit with the knife. His eyes water and focus hungrily on the task. Clancy opens the door and pretends to be searching in the car for the money. Without putting her seatbelt on, she slides the key into the ignition. The car screeches as she leaves the station behind her; in the rear-view mirror she spies the policeman running to his car. Clancy diverts her route to travel down a closed road, still repeatedly checking the rear-view mirror for the possibility of flashing police lights. She imagines everything going horribly wrong. The hitch-hiker's mouth forms the shape of a word, but he says nothing. Clancy begins to wish that he would talk. The car rattles as she forces the gear stick into fifth; the dial of the speedometer refuses to waiver above seventy miles per hour.

Concentrating on looking for the bright blue signs that will announce Myrtle Point, she stares ahead to the iciness of the water that will chill her skin. Quarter of a mile before her destination, Clancy brings the car to a halt at the side of the road. The stranger reclines further back in the seat and shuffles his feet against the floor.

'This is as far as we go,' Clancy declares.

She waits for him to leave, but he does not. The road is quiet and the inside car light fades. Clancy looks at the eerily glowing digital clock as the minutes slowly pass by. Eventually he picks up his bag and without a word of thanks climbs out of the car and walks away.

'Weirdo,' Clancy says to herself. However, she compulsively watches him as he disappears into the distance.

At the destination, Clancy's red shoes scud across the path as if their soles were temporary. Her shoulders are hunched, replicating the image of a tortoise carrying its heavy shell. Her eyes do not need to focus. She has walked this path many times before. It was their place and now she cannot even remember the sound of Choisin's voice. As children they had spread picnic rugs over the grass and later they had come here separately with boyfriends. When she reaches the cliff top, she slides out of her shoes. Her arms tremble slightly as she leans over the edge. The olive shaped eyes are closed, until she finally opens them. In front of her the deep pool of water is patched with pockets of aquamarine and navy blue. A cluster of rocks juts out like a row of teeth encased in the mouth of a great white shark. Choisin was the twin who could swim.

Clancy decides to jump after slowly counting to three. 'One, two... three.' She surprises herself, immediately flinging her body into the rushing air. Her arms flail ungracefully above her head. She expects her life to flash through her mind, just like the attestations of plane crash survivors. Instead all she can think about is Joel with his hands all over that girl. Why on earth had she not ended the relationship?

The cold water smacks viciously against her entering toes, before bruising her legs with the impact. Sour water fills her lungs as she tumbles into the current. Clancy chokes up the liquid as she returns briefly to the surface. She can see nothing; her eyes are stinging with saltiness. Her arms bump against the rock and she dips completely under the water. She gasps for a breath of air and she flaps her hands like the paws of a drowning dog. She realises that she does not want to die like this — at least not today.

The waves break on her again and she submerges into their clutches.

Underneath the water, the hitchhiker who had followed her, spirals around until Clancy appears almost as if she was a vision, still and tranquil with only her flowing hair betraying movement. The heaviness of his clothes is forgotten as he wraps his arms around her. His legs kick manically as he brings them upwards.

It takes several efforts, but he finally hauls the limp body on to the top of the rock. Clancy's skin is tinged with a violent blue hue. Segments of a first aid course flash though his mind as he rests his lips against hers. Nothing happens. His hands press repeatedly against her chest and he breathes into her mouth. Her body jerks; frothy pink sputum is expelled with a spluttering cough. Clancy's eyelashes flutter and she opens her eyes briefly. He shakes Clancy gently in an attempt to keep her conscious. The nearest hospital is over ten miles away and his mobile phone has been rendered inoperable by the water. Under the rapidly blackening sky, he carries the doll-like body up the hill, unaware of the stones crushing into the bare soles of his feet.

Train

Jack Crittenden

'Doors closing, please stand clear.'
Heavy footfalls collide with the crisp
Hiss of the doors,
A headless voice grumbles from
Just over my left shoulder,
Just out of sight.

The myriad settle.
Shuffling together, squeezing one more in —
Irksome, awkward, uncomfortably close.
The noise level lowers as the passengers do.

Morning tabloids rustle;
Once, twice, the pages shaken out.
Suits fall away, minds grope
For meaning in the early morning.
Transcending their metal conveyor, they flee
To distant horizons and other people's lives.
An old couple murmur softly to each other's memories.

The air is close.
Shirts stick, slick,
With sweat steaming

From contact with worn blue upholstery.
The sun pierces the faded tinting.
No breath of air in this ageing iron horse.

We descend into darkness
With a woosh!
Shoulders slump with relief.
The student glances furtively from his reader
As other youths, mp3s firmly wired in,
Peek shyly, sizing one another up.
Eyes dart swiftly back to nothingness —
Spotted!
Cheeks flush as I try to melt into my seat.
Trouble is, I'm succeeding.

'Dong ding dang.'
Silent sufferers start,
Reveries shattered as
Monotony drones out the next destination.
Deep in the bowels of the earth we make our way
Ever onwards, rolling rattles reverberating,
Fluoros flickering as we flash past in the black,
Stationary.
Bursting once more into the light the train
Clatters onto the bridge.
The carriage powers through the steel cathedral,

Shadows flash past
Like the cars that flit around us,
Cleaner fish trailing a silver shark that
Pushes ever onwards through the summer morning.

Blue green sparkles as
We punch through pylons that call us home.
Mighty sails are hoisted to our left, immobile.
Obelisks of glass and metal crowd in on every side,
Enveloping us with harsh lines and glittering shadows.
Gone is the warm embrace of our riveted womb with its flowing
    lines,
Replaced by clawing talons
Nails jagged,
They rake the heavens.

My heavy footfalls collide with the crisp hiss of the doors,
I plunge from the tin cigar onto the platform; hot wind parches
    my aching throat as I suck it in
Desperately
Drawn by an invisible force —
My feet take up the burden of the carriage, and I push on
    through.

Stained-glass Windows

Simone De Simone

The window cast a soft light across the damp room
and reminded me of when we lay scattered on the floor
like shattered pieces of glass,
different colours all mixed into a blurred and dappled pile,
and we just lay there
a broken tangle.

Slowly,
when we needed to move again
one by one
we collected the broken pieces that once were us
and alone and lonely, we attempted to piece ourselves back
    together.

Once we thought we were whole again
we looked down
and realised,
we were the pieces of each other,
glued back together stronger than before
a stained-glass window to filter the light
made out of pieces of you and me.

The window is still there
and I still carry a piece of each of you with me
and forever you carry a broken piece of me,
a silent bond never to be broken
a bond held together by what we once lost.

One of Many Days in Oncology

Nathan Droguett

Sitting alone staring motionless in all directions at white
Sunlight shining past me from behind while I'm held tight
So comfortable, sinking my aching body into the soft red
reclining chair
As the cannula is reinserted for the third time, I gasp in despair
Finally, a drop of blood in the plastic transparent tube
One tiny step for today's work, still not destroying my decent
mood
I relax, lie back and take notice of my boring forearms
Where there used to be a maze of veins, now just small circular
scars

The angel rushes over as I wince in unbearable pain
The needle slipped, my arm swells and I try to remain
contained
After another attempt it successfully yet slowly slides into my
bicep
The continuously moving poison enters swiftly and I'm content
Closing my heavy though wary eyes, I begin to dream of a
better time
Sinking through grains of sand, hearing waves crash, absorbing
sunshine

Running my fingers through straight damp hair and smiling at
freedom
Deciding what to do the day after next; the choice, so random

Suddenly awakened into harsh reality with a different
unbearable pain
Remembering quickly that each day it occurs with this poison
strain
I tense my weak arm and with the other I wave around for an
angel to see
None in sight, all busy, racing around for other people like me
I'm desperate, the intense throbbing pain gets the best of me; I
shed a tear
No one around to help; suddenly, a deep sense of fear
I recover, clench my fist and fight through my physical stress
Copy what the angel did yesterday, turn it off and regain my
breath

She arrives with a smile and everything I feel subsides
All is gone, peace is retained, she is the moon and the pains are
the tides
I'm comforted; reassured the chemicals will be diluted
Thankfully she knows exactly what I wanted but more impor-
tantly much needed
It slowly but surely begins to reenter my bloodstream

I feel it, bearably painful, moving along my body as though
visually seen
I try and relax, not think about it and look at the time
It's been eight hours but it's the fifth and final similar day in
this cycle of mine

I get up to go to the bathroom for the ninth time today
Unplugging the machine, untangling the tubes, beginning to
walk away
I take the cold metal pole holding the poison by my side as I
reach the door
Awkward wheels moving in all random directions, getting
stuck on the floor
With one numb arm and the other completely connected
Business is done one handed; over time the skills have been
perfected
At last! It's over for the week I hear the machine screeching
Pure bliss and silence enters my body — a truly beautiful
feeling

Grateful the weekend has begun, a few days of rest is what I
need
Getting me disconnected and ready to leave; 'as soon as
possible,' I plead
The needles and tape removed from my colourless skin
Thrown away, out of plain sight into a special disposable bin

I get warm, grab a hand to help me stand and my frail legs
hardly hold
'Get home', 'drink fluids', 'get into bed and relax' are the things
I'm told
I thank my angels, reassure I'll be back next week and give
them a warm forced smile
Taking small slow steps to the car, I will get there; just might
take a while

Not Without Vision

Christine Greaves

*Blind! What of that? Man has five senses... He had five arrows
in his quiver; well, he has shot one away, and four remain. My
dear, an enemy is not disarmed because he's lost one arrow out
of five.*

Pygmalion and Galatea by W.S. Gilbert (1871)

Several pages turn, bumps are deftly skimmed, fingers rise and fall like
the pressure applied to piano keys without the entanglement of sound.

The second year of her life dispensed the illness that closed Amy's
eyes and ears, plunging her into the naïve insensibility of a newborn.
They labelled it acute congestion of the brain. No one foretold that
she should never see or hear again.

Some say that a mother's finest achievement is the raising of her
children. When I classify my earliest impressions of Amy's disabil-
ities, I find myself glowing in the pride that I gave my daughter the
gift of passing from night into day, from isolation to companionship,
knowledge, love.

***

Autumn, 1859

Dear diary,

Follow thee in thy ovation splendid,
Thine almoner, the wind, scatters the gold leaves!

I have decided to treat Amy (now five) like a two-year-old child. I asked myself, 'How does a healthy child learn language?' The response was simple, 'By imitation.' The child comes into the world with the ability to learn, provided he is given sufficient outward stimulus. He sees people do things, and he tries to do them. He hears others speak, and he tries to speak. But long before he utters his first word, he understands what is said to him.

I have since devised a method to teach Amy to communicate. I shall talk into her hands as a mother talks into her baby's ears; I shall assume that she has the healthy child's capacity for assimilation, I shall use complete sentences in talking to her and complete the meaning with gestures when necessity requires it; but I shall not attempt to keep her mind fixed on any one thing. There is not a soul in this part of the world to whom I can go for advice in this endeavour. The only thing for me to do in a perplexity is to advance, and learn by inevitably making mistakes.

My Amy is a frolicking stream, sashaying past the banks of sorrowful shadows. I arrived at this portraiture the day Amy and I visited the local river. As the rivulet gushed over her right hand, I traced 'w-a-t-e-r' onto her left, first slowly, then rapidly. She stood motionless, her vacant eyes riveted upon the rhythm of my fingers. It was as if she had been handed the key to unlock the enigma of language. Vaulting from foot to foot, she splashed water in abundance. The word had awakened her soul, given her vision, set her free! There were barriers still, it is true, but barriers that could be swept away.

Spring, 1859

Dear diary,

Broad-sowing, cheerful, plenteous,
Quickening underneath the mould
Grains beyond the price of gold.

My beloved continues to manifest the same eagerness to learn as that day in Autumn. Every moment is exhausted by her incremental and insatiable quest for knowledge. It is splendid to feel that you are indispensable to another's evolvement. Amy's zeal transcends her across sundry obstacles that would be our undoing if we stopped to explicate everything. What would happen, do you think, if someone were to measure our intelligence by our ability to define the commonest words we use? I fear that if I were put to such a test I should be consigned to a school for the feeble-minded.

I truly feel that nothing crushes one's development more effectually than blackboard exercises, all erased within minutes. Language should not be associated with endless hours in school, baffling questions of grammar, or with anything that is the antithesis of joy. Everything we have seen and heard is in the mind somewhere. It may be too disconcerting to be recognisable, but it there all the same, like the landscape we lose in the deepening twilight.

Summer, 1859

Dear diary,

The leaves drift down, the green grows brown
And tears with smiles are blended;

A twilight hour and a treasured flower, —
And now the poem is ended

This year has seen Amy learn to see not with her eyes, but through the inner faculty to serve which eyes were given us. She responds quickly to the gentle pressure of affection, the pat of approval, the firm motion of command, the disparate variations of the almost infinite language of the psyche.

She is my treasured flower.

***

Amy is now seventeen years old. She derives great pleasure from reading to me that which she has composed in Braille. The bumpy incidents of our daily lives pass around her unobserved, but she has enough detailed acquaintance with the quest that is life to keep her perspective from being inherently deficient.

On many levels, I have transformed Amy's limitations into resplendent privileges, and encouraged her to stroll in defiance of the shadow cast by her deprivation. In turn, she has awarded me the finest fulfilment a mother can boast in today's unforgiving society — the acceptance of wisdom. Her peers see Amy not as possessing the intrinsic helplessness so often connoted with loss of sight and hearing, but rather her innate capacity to nullify this disability and find her place in the community with the same degree of success as everyone else.

A Full Circle

Zainab Rifaath Anver

Perveen Jeet awakened to the sharp sound of metal on marble. She peeked cautiously through the narrow slits of her eyes to see her husband Sohail had dropped his belt on the bedroom floor, the guilty buckle caught red-handed and shamefaced creating the racket. Sohail was running late and couldn't afford to tiptoe around her, but Perveen didn't mind. She closed her eyes, pretending that sleep still rendered her unconscious and oblivious to the noise, and waited patiently until the rustle of papers and footsteps ceased, confirming that Sohail was out the front door. Just to be certain, she edged surreptitiously to the window and peered slowly from behind the curtain, watching for his car to back out of the drive way. Like a secret agent in a Bond film.

'Okay. Right. The bathroom needs a good wash. I can leave the vacuuming for later and I'll start preparing lunch early. We haven't had a good curry in a while,' she said to herself, tilting her head left and right as she pondered her schedule for the day. 'But I should do the laundry first.' Perveen delighted in starching her husband's sarongs excessively while doing the laundry, so much so that Sohail had received several paper cuts from his crisp garment over the years. Sometimes these cheap thrills were all she asked for in a day.

'Maybe I can take some chicken vindaloo to Harun. I bet he hasn't eaten a good meal in days. Then I'd better do it soon before Sohail comes back,' she mused, continuing her earlier train of thought.

Walking down to the kitchen, Perveen barely noticed her opulent surroundings. Gliding down the wide, winding staircase as if in a sleepwalk, she was no longer mesmerized by the view from the eastbound French doors that opened out to the spacious and well manicured lawns with a small cupid water fountain in the centre. The sunlight poured into the living room downstairs casting a majestic golden glow, illuminating the pictures on the walls and the cream coloured sofa sets. The interior of the house was so unlike her home in India, and evinced Perveen's great panache in decorating (with inspiration of course from Oprah's home renovation shows). For that, she had been the envy of many in the large Indian community, of which they liked to consider themselves a vital part. Over time however, she felt no satisfaction in catching envious glances from them: there was no flattery in having them emulate her style within a week or two. What was all this luxury when there was no one to enjoy it with?

Hours passed and it was soon close to twelve in the afternoon. Perveen was still cloaked in her robe, her hair disarrayed in a poor semblance of the plait she wore the night before. Her bowl of Coco Pops for breakfast lay forgotten and soggy, growing more uninviting by the minute. She stared out the window above the sink, looking but not really seeing until her eyes focused. She realised Michael, the neighbour across the road — who never missed an opportunity to tell her how exotic he thought Indian women were while staring shamelessly at her plump breasts — was waving to her while watering his petunias. Once again, he was wearing nothing but those too-tight shorts that bordered on indecent and made Perveen feel like she was sinning just looking at him. She abruptly turned her face as if she hadn't seen him and went back to stirring the pan of chicken vindaloo, letting it simmer. She watched the steam rise, and let out a resigned sigh, once again taking stock of her life.

Perveen married at the age of twenty-three. It was considered old according to the parochial Indian customs that so dictated her life — close to a woman's expiration date on the marriage market, in fact. It was an arranged marriage, one that was most profitable to her. Sohail came from a rich and well-respected family of the Brahmin caste and he was well qualified to leave India and work abroad. It was Perveen's good looks, her fair skin — a quality that was so sought after amongst many in her community — that recommended her to Sohail's family. To Sohail's family, there was the added bonus that she appeared somewhat modernised, she had been educated and worked as an administrative assistant in a reputable architectural firm in Delhi. But not too modernised that she would give trouble to her in-laws. No, Perveen was the perfect daughter-in-law. When Sohail's mother, Nandita, subtly suggested to her that at twenty-four her biological clock was ticking and she had not a moment to lose in getting pregnant, Perveen spoke to her husband about having children. Perveen's status as a dutiful daughter-in-law was elevated as she succeeded in producing a son at her first try. After all, what good is a baby-making machine when it doesn't produce the best quality goods?

It was not long after, that Sohail's engineering company transferred him to Sydney, where Perveen was at last rid of her mother-in-law's subtle but constant demands — although not completely free from the watchful eyes and gossiping tongues of their Indian community. She and Sohail had raised their son Harun with the same Indian values and culture as they had grown up with. But they also took pride in their standing as a modernised, open-minded and liberal family who integrated with Australian society.

While other families only permitted their sons and daughters to befriend other Indians, Sohail and Perveen were not as strict.

'And look where it got us!' Sohail had once shouted bitterly. The memory of that fight lingered painfully. When Harun finished school, Sohail and Perveen were so proud. They announced it to everyone gleefully, eager for praise that their son had successfully secured a position to study Medical Science at the University of Sydney. He would be the first in their community to do so and Sohail and Perveen planned a gala event at their huge house to celebrate — in other words to tastefully parade — their triumph.

Perveen winced as she recalled that afternoon. Harun walked in the front doors, flagged by waiters bringing in the catered Indian food. Enticing smells of hot lamb biryani wafted in the air. Even their Australian neighbours had complimented the smells, hoping for an invite.

Harun found his mother talking with one of the waiters and decided to drop his bombshell on her then. He announced that he was going to move out to live with a girl in an apartment near campus. He swore they were just friends, but what did it matter? He was going to live with a girl, and not a proper Indian girl either, for what good Indian girl would live with a boy until she was married? No, he was going to live with a white girl, and he expected his mother to break the news gently to Sohail. Perveen had the sense to carry on the charade of that perfect family that had no dirty laundry to air and the party went off without a hitch. It did for the Jeets, at least. The shameless Mrs Sharmah, who devoured the food with such uncouth zest, aimed some of the thick gravy at her white *salwar kameez* instead of her mouth, while her husband fell asleep on the couch in the corner of the room, snoring loudly with drool dribbling carelessly down his double chin which was thick with stubble, and the often ebullient Mr Kapoor started to make a nuisance of himself, his garrulous nature allowing him to dominate the conversation.

When the last of the guests had left and the waiters had been paid at past twelve in the night, Perveen decided now was as good a time as any to break the news to her husband. Unfortunately Harun, thinking his father had already been enlightened, spilled the beans rather callously. Predictably, it had ended badly. Sohail had declared that Harun was no son of his and if he was so eager to leave home he might as well do it now. Perveen had wailed and begged her husband fruitlessly to take back his words. Harun was their son, their only child. He made a mistake sure, but what were his parents there for if not to guide him to the right path from now? That had only provoked Sohail to unleash his fury on his wife instead.

'This is all your doing!' he shouted. 'You're the one who insisted we accept the offer to come here! I was happy to stay in Bombay with my family. Your parents were also close by in Delhi. Huh! Harun would have grown up with family values, he would have had plenty of people watching out for him. But you insisted we come here, let him get influenced by these things he sees on TV.' Spit sprayed from his mouth, showering her furiously blinking eyes. His voice which was usually so carefully modulated, and his accent which he normally cultivated to sound as Australian as he could manage, now reverberated so loudly through the vast emptiness of the house and sounded so Indian, it was as if they had never left Bombay twenty years ago.

'Okay, baba, calm down please. The neighbours will hear all your talk. What could we have done, huh? You know even the Jaspereet family, they were so strict with their kids, they went astray anyway. That daughter of theirs married a Christian, and then she also converted. You can't control these things,' she lamented, hitting her forehead with the heel of her palm.

What will everyone say? Perveen wondered inwardly, releasing a long strangled sigh. They've all been waiting for something like this to happen. No one could stand to see us so happy and successful. Everyone enjoys a good show of how the mighty have fallen...

Aloud she said, 'We can take care of this, we can talk to him... '

She was cut off abruptly by her husband's incredulous scoff. 'Talk to him? I will never speak to that traitor again. He will never set foot in this house and you will never see him again. How could he tarnish our family name like this? Not a regard to what we have sacrificed to give him a good education, a good life in a country like this. In India he wouldn't have been so lucky! And he completely disregards our way of life, our culture and traditions! And all for what? His freedom? Or this girl?'

Every time Perveen opened her mouth to interject on her son's behalf, Sohail unleashed more, his tone becoming more and more venomous and his anger increasingly directed at her as well as their son. He had never been a laconic man. Perveen tried to tune out most of it but caught his ceremonious grand finale: 'No, we should never have come here, Perveen, you should have been happy in India instead of nagging me to come here!'

Of course it was all her fault. Had she stayed in India, the butterfly effect would have led to a completely different life, a perfect life, one where every attempt to shun that part of her that she so despised would have succeeded, where every new beginning would have granted her the better life she craved, where she — not customs or elders — controlled her life.

With that, he stormed off, slamming their bedroom door behind him, leaving Perveen to tidy up the living room, sobbing softly to herself, almost like a hum.

From then on, both husband and wife were careful never to mention Harun's name or anything that might remotely remind them of the existence of their son. It was as if almost twenty years of their lives had been wiped clean in one evening. They endured their community's gossip with good grace, tempted at first to lie and say he had gone to Harvard or some other prestigious university outside of Australia. But they knew that would never suffice. There were far too many Indians carefully positioned in all parts of the world, all related to each other in some bizarre web, that the truth would come out and exacerbate their shame. But for Perveen, she could not bear the separation from her only son, and whenever her husband was out of the house she would scurry to the phone, eager to hear Harun's voice. She would still cook for him, taking the food to meet Harun at a park. She couldn't quite bring herself to enter his apartment, her love and acceptance of her son not spanning to include his choice of lifestyle .

Perveen snapped out of her reverie when she realised she had kept the pan on the fire far too long and the gravy had simmered leaving a thick dark brown coating on the non-stick surface. She cursed in Hindi and went upstairs to take a shower, her son still deep in her thoughts.

At least he's happy, he's having a good life. Sohail, Nandita, they can all blame me, but what more can a mother ask for than her son's happiness? It's more than I can say for myself, she thought bitterly.

Her relationship with her husband had been no different to other newlyweds' who had arranged marriages. They got married and fell in love later. That was the only acceptable order of things even for those more modern. Everyone would comment on how in love they appeared to be. It would seem that Sohail was affectionate to her, he would buy her the very best of saris, Indian jewellery, branded Western clothes. He would take her out to dinner just the two of them, he would hold her hand in public and always hold doors open for her. Amidst such a patriarchal community where most males were such chauvinists, gentleman-like behaviour could easily be construed for love. And certainly they did love each other. Over the years they had become quite comfortable around each other, so attuned to each others' quirky habits and learning to tolerate those habits that they could not force the other to get rid of.

But were they ever in love with each other? Perveen couldn't tell. What is love anyway, she wondered while massaging the shampoo so vigorously into her scalp that it started to burn. I never felt any of those heart flutters or electric shocks, whatever they call it in the books and movies.

Regardless of the nature of their relationship, they had been comfortable in each other's presence. Now, being in the same room with the other was always a torment, as if a painful reminder of what had happened in that house mere months ago. Their relationship had slowly deteriorated. They spoke only about important matters, like community functions, bills and other household affairs that could not be avoided or conveyed on a post-it note stuck on the refrigerator door. Sex had become something of a chore, each going through the motions without any feeling and only at Sohail's initiative. He would come home and ask if she were sleepy, that was his way of letting her know his intentions. They would stand at their respective sides of the bed, concentrating hard on removing their own clothes, careful not to look at each other, the light switched off so that neither could see each other's unflattering floppy bits, a hallmark of their age. It would be over in minutes, no talk, no sound except for the creaking of the mattress, no caressing, just him on top of her. It wasn't long before they gave up even going through the motions.

Eventually conversation was also limited to the barest essentials.

What a change, Perveen mused as hot tears of shame cascaded down her already wet cheeks. He used to talk to me about every-thing that happened at work. It was never interesting but he would confide in me at least. Now nothing, it's as if I don't exist.

The hot water gushed over her but Perveen could no longer feel anything, her body so numb with a pain that threatened to overwhelm her. It seeped into her like sugar melting in a cup of hot tea. How long she sat there for, curled up into a ball and weeping until the hot water ran out and was replaced by icy cold, she did not know. Her fingers were all shriveled up like raisins from being soaked so long, and her body was stiff. She examined her soggy skin with detached eyes: she had stopped feeling womanly and desired a long time ago. The tears had stopped flowing but she still hummed tearfully as if the sound of her grief comforted her in her solitude. She remained in a foetal position, thinking to herself and suddenly all her plans for the day seemed irrelevant. Anger replaced her sadness and soon turned to determination.

'All these years I've been looking after everyone else, I've always put my needs last and now look, I'm all alone, no one cares about me and certainly no one's looking after me,' she muttered bitterly to herself, now staring at her reflection in the mirror without really seeing herself.

Her eyes slowly focused to absorb the pitiful image that confronted her: red puffy eyes and a nose that had swollen to twice its original size. 'If no one is going to bother about you, then you might as well start,' she asserted with more force, as if her alter ego was urging the spineless doormat that was her old self. As if in the seconds it took to turn her sadness around, she had miraculously transformed. Behold the new Perveen, who cared about herself though no one else did. Just like when people make New Year's resolutions and actually stick to them, their lives miraculously improve starting from the first of January. Perveen had had plenty of new beginnings but it had never really been the first of January for her.

All dressed and as presentable as she could muster, Perveen soon found herself at the train station, as if her feet had willed her there without her mind being included in the plan. This was where all her epiphanies took place: while riding on trains. Here she knew she could escape everything that weighed on her shoulders. She sat herself down by the window, unsure of what destination was listed on her ticket. A feeling of peace swept over her like a warm blanket. She examined the faces on the platform, wondered what their lives were like, what thoughts were swimming through their pretty heads at that precise moment. She heard the doors close shut and the monotone voice over the PA system announce it was an express train to goodness knows where. She smelled a waft of curry and felt her warm blanket being ripped from her. She was about to turn her head around to find the culprit; who dared present however subtle a reminder of the life she was desperate to escape?

Of course he would come and sit here, it's like Indians attract Indians, Perveen thought furiously while purposefully trying to avoid his keen gaze. Well I won't encourage him. As could be predicted he would seat himself right in front of her.

'Wery hawt today?' the man commented uselessly but added a question mark at the end to prompt her.

She took a quick glance at him unwillingly but it was enough to confirm her disdain of him. He fit the stereotype Perveen had in mind of the Indian who didn't come from money, the worst kind. He was attired in a mismatched suit which was a size too big for him so that he had to fold the sleeves of his jacket and the hems at his feet. Instead of proper men's shoes to match the suit, he wore a bulky pair of sports shoes, the laces of which were half untied. He could look striking, had he taken better care of his appearance and not greased his hair. Perveen tried not to look at his open mouth into which he was speedily shoving forks-full of fried soggy chips drenched in what smelled like butter chicken gravy. Where on earth did he find that concoction?

Why do people feel the need to clutter space in the universe with meaningless chatter? Silence is more comfortable. I should have sat somewhere else, she fumed inwardly.

The stranger on the train was quick to decipher that Perveen was not in an exceptionally chatty mood that morning. He tried what he thought was a different tactic. He shifted in his seat moving the wound-up rope he carried to the floor so he could take up the whole seat.

'Going somewhere?'

'No I just like riding on trains,' she could not help answering.

He looked stung for a second but regained his composure. Perveen realised he thought she was being sarcastic and immediately felt bad.

Well at least it might get him to shut up.

'Ah, I see the sea!' he exclaimed philosophically, pointing his fork at her and involuntarily flinging gravy at her. Perveen ducked to the side and just missed it. Her patience with this man was clearly being tested.

'Trouble in paradise, huh?'

It irritated her the way he spoke, emphasising the letter 'a' and pronouncing 'w' in the place of 'v'. She looked at him indignantly but he appeared unperturbed by her death-glare and boldly clarified, 'You know... trouble in the lowe department?'

'Trouble? No, no trouble.' She was careful to enunciate clearly and speak with an Australian accent, a subtle hint at his incorrect pronunciation, which unfortunately slid right over his head.

'But you're lonely, no?' he said sympathetically.

'No, just trying to find some alone time, you know, so I can think in peace.'

'So you're not running away, then? Because running away only binds you to "it" furthermore.' His tone was meant to be grave but came out comical. He was on a roll here. 'You know why? Because running away is only the symptom of a problem and it only asserts the *existence* of your problem. So, what you must do is find out what you are hiding from and why. That is the key,' he finished proudly.

Perveen frowned deeply, her patience for the stranger running exceptionally low the closer he hit home. How was it that he knew exactly which chords to strike at? Some part of her wanted to spill her whole sob story and it battled with the other part of her that wanted to fabricate a new life for herself which would feel all the more tangible if this stranger was a witness to it. Even if it was a farce.

'Look I'm not pulling your leg here,' she started but she didn't miss him quickly look down at his leg, puzzled as if really checking that she was not doing anything to his leg. She smiled despite herself. 'I really am just riding on trains for the heck of it. It might sound strange to you but I am so easily amused by these small things.'

He looked like he was having trouble understanding her thick accent, accentuated for his benefit. But he relished in the fact that this beautiful stranger was actually giving him the time of day.

'No, really, I get a hoot from watching Funniest Home Videos on TV. And you know yesterday when I was getting out of the car park at the mall I got a kick from watching this family there, mother, father and two daughters, who were rushing to their car to get out of the parking lot before they had to pay extra for parking. I could feel the excitement, the electricity within them. They were full of life and silent laughter.' She paused to see if he was still listening, unaware that her own voice sounded like she was reading a story. 'It was like

182

they were in a race in a video game called The Big Bad World. They were being chased by time, and the greedy parking machines were ready to swallow up their shiny gold two dollar coin, like that was the treasure that they needed to keep. And I was so caught up in it, urging them on as if I controlled the joy stick to the video game, and cheered silently as they got past the ticket barrier.'

She stopped herself from admitting aloud that she wished fervently to control the joy stick of her own life. How different it would be.

But would it really? she thought bitterly. I got what I wanted, didn't I? I wanted a man who could go abroad. I refused all the other proposals for this. I chose this and now what? Nothing went as I planned it.

Frustration consumed her as she realised she could not blame anyone else. She was no ordinary suburban housewife who could blame her downward spiral on circumstance and life. No, she had made her own bed and was made to lie in it, much to her chagrin. There was no fun not being able to blame others for her misfortunes. After all, she thought she had paid more than her share of life's taxes. Shouldn't she be granted that one small concession? She could blame God but she was afraid to. She was Hindu and a strong believer in karma. God would get her back for it somehow, as if this payback wasn't enough for whatever atrocities she had committed in her past life. Slowly, her new found optimism from this morning slipped away like a silky cloth disrobing her, leaving her raw pain bare, no longer masked by beautiful garments and false hope. The stranger excused himself at the next station.

Well he obviously got more than he bargained for! Perveen thought with a grim smile that didn't reach her eyes. A voice in her head added a moment later, Don't we all?

She lingered on the train without paying attention to her surroundings until she realised that the train she was on was a city circle link. She was going round and round in circles. It was like God was not going to let her escape. She felt as though her heart dipped to her stomach as another epiphany hit her with the force of a speeding train.

Maybe he's right. Running away doesn't work that way. I should have known all along, its basic Hindu philosophy after all! she thought. The signs were always there, why didn't I see them?

Perveen's life before she got married flashed in her mind like a motion picture. She realised that she had tried to run away from a part of herself, her identity and it was that desire that propelled her to accept Sohail's marriage proposal. Perveen's desperate endeavours to control her life only resulted in it spiralling wildly out of control. When she moved to Sydney she thought she could find herself, but instead she was lost further in a web of confusion and pretence. Every fruitless attempt to denounce that critical part of herself had simply bound her to it ever more irrevocably.

And if she was being completely honest with herself, her train ride was not for mere merriment. She just needed a place to think about her next move, her next big escape to find herself. But she knew now no matter where she ran away to she would not find herself because she had left Perveen behind in the very first place she tried to escape. And she knew that was where she needed to be right now.

She laughed her dulcet laugh that had not been used in a long while, at the irony that was her life.

It's like my life has really come around in a full circle, she mused.

And for the first time, Perveen felt like the first of January was right around the corner.

Stationary

Hannah Croke

Suburban station workers meander
like country folk on a Sunday,
unfazed by the arrival
of an approaching train.

Perhaps it is the suddenness of all that sky
slowing them to a rural pace,
the long curving tracks like dirt roads
dry and exposed, following
the sound of waiting,
waiting for the rain or the train

while people stand with their long shadows
like idle cattle chewing cud.

Roach's Inheritance

Raymond Baltas

in the distance

many men lie dead three feet

deep in ancient soil

numbering in something

like the

population of mega-cities

tenfold

while above,

cockroaches

dance the dance

of evolution on

their graves,

their numbers now

bursting forth

from the depths

of the earth's dankest

caverns,

outnumbering the dead

beneath,

one hundredfold.

Fading

Joan Short

The second last time my mother came to visit us she got off the train looking crushed and confused.

'Why not the plane, Mum?' I took her bony arm to guide her to the car.

'Easier by train. Just catch the bus to Wagga, train to here. Easy. Never liked the thought of flying. Can't trust pilots... '

My husband Rob picked up her case. It looked hollow and slack like a deflated balloon.

'Traveling light, May?'

All she'd thought to bring were an old pair of sandals and the daggiest nightdress I'd ever seen. We had to stop on the way home to get her some new clothes. She'd forgotten just about all her social graces but we couldn't buy those. It seemed she never went anywhere when she was at home. Since Dad had died all her food had to be delivered by the owner of the Bird's Supermarket. People in Clement hardly ever saw her, and most of her friends were either dead or had given up on her. Can't say I blame them, and anyway, what could I do about it?

You know your mother is going to die. You're born with that sort of information imprinted onto your brain. When you're a kid you hear about old people dying. Like old Mrs Carruthers next door; one day she was sitting in her floral chair talking to someone that no one else could see, but she seemed happy enough and the next morning she was dead.

'Died in her sleep,' Mum said. 'A real blessing.'

'But why is it a blessing?' I asked Mum, over and over. 'Isn't it better to be not dead?'

Mum never gave me a proper answer to this question. I know now that there is no answer, but I couldn't see any advantage in being dead. Heaven seemed to me to be a pale place. Our animals died too. We found Ned, our old border collie, dead in the paddock one morning after he'd been missing for a couple of days. Mum couldn't tell me if there was a dog heaven or not. I don't think she knew, or else she was too kind to tell me if there wasn't. If there'd been an animal heaven there would have been other animals there like the odd dead sheep, and the birds we'd find lying around the paddocks. This heaven would have been a crowded place, even without the rabbits that Dad either shot or infected with myxomatosis. My questions drove Mum mad.

'Don't know where Helen gets her funny ideas, Eric,' I heard her say one day when she didn't know I was just outside the kitchen door.

I never had the guts to challenge Mum too much, not worth my while. She had a way of making me feel guilty and she saw to that from my earliest days. Probably programmed it in at birth. Used her sick headaches as a weapon in our war of nerves. She lurched from one headache to another, and whenever we had a family outing, or if the slightest thing went wrong, Mum would collapse in a darkened room with a cool cloth over her eyes. Dad and I would creep around, hoping she wouldn't call out for us.

'Eric, Eric... '

Dad would creep into the room with another damp cloth and a glass of water and maybe some headache powder.

'May, love... we're being as quiet as we can.'

No way I'd ever have told anyone this, but I loved those nights because it meant Dad would have to cook.

'What'll we have, Helen? Reckon we could manage one of my famous fry-ups?'

He'd cook bacon, eggs, sausages, tomatoes and toast with butter dripping off it. More butter than Mum ever let me have. I loved butter, even loved making it.

'Keep that churn going, Helen. Faster,' Dad would say.

When the butter was firm I'd decorate the pats with lines and crosses and a prominent 'HA' to remind everyone of my artistic leanings.

On those nights we'd have dinner in front of the fire with our plates on our laps, and if Dad was feeling extra generous he'd have a beer and I'd have a huge glass of fifty-fifty cordial. Even our old cat Jacko would move closer to the fire and purr more loudly than usual. He didn't have Mum there to worry about the cat hairs all over the mat.

Poor Dad, he loved the farm. He stayed there a lot of the time. Town was just not for him. He had a feeling for the land and he'd find any excuse not to come back into town for the night — lambing time, an early start, too tired — and the farm was only about eight miles away. I missed him but I don't know that Mum did. She'd insisted that we move to town when I was about ten.

'You need a good schooling to get ahead in life, Helen. Don't get stuck here like I did.'

I've often wondered how she felt when Dad died. She didn't want to know the neighbours who came to see her afterwards.

'What a terrible thing May... Poor Eric... imagine having a heart attack way out there on his own... and poor Helen...'

Well, poor Helen. I only wanted to be on my own and no one gave me time to really think about it. And there was the end of school exams to think about. I just had to matriculate.

I don't remember much about the funeral but I heard the mocking crows and the wind making the casuarina trees groan. And nothing much changed between Mum and me.

I always found it hard to believe my parents were happy. I hardly ever saw or heard them laughing together. Dad was quiet and calm and seemed like he could put up with anything. He had to be like that, I suppose. Mum spent so much time alone, either in the house doing her incessant cleaning or on the side veranda reading. She wouldn't speak to anyone when she was there, and I often wondered how she could say she was reading when she was staring out into space, at nothing. At least she was quiet enough then, but she didn't have a veranda like this when we moved into town.

It was always... 'Helen, hang up your clothes... pick up your shoes... feed the chooks...'

On and on until my ears ached. When she was on the veranda I had a chance to lie on my bedroom floor and read my latest library book.

The last time my mother came to visit us was the time we realised that she couldn't look after herself any more. The doctor in Clement rang to tell us this just before Christmas.

'Helen, she can't manage on her own any more. Hardly even gets out of bed some days. I'll organise a nursing home assessment. They'll contact your doctor in Sydney.'

More guilt, more remorse and emotional self-flagellation. I'd always hated my visits back to Clement after Dad died, and felt more comfortable with my head in the sand. Dr Brendon had done all she could; even managed to make Mum take her pills most days which was good as Mum had no friends in town now.

We took her to the Azalea House Nursing Home in Sydney — 'The Warren' Rob called it. Visiting the place was a real chore. At first she'd fold her arms and turn her back to me. She hated me for moving her away from Clement, but the more her dementia took over the calmer she became. May blended in so well with all the other old ladies often I didn't recognise her. She hardly looked anything like her younger self.

We used to drag the kids along to visit but they hated it and whinged the whole time.

'The place smells Mum. She doesn't even know who we are.'

Susie usually took a book to read but that was only for show so she wouldn't have to talk to anyone. Sometimes Mum would look at James and reach for his hand and call him Eric. I'd tell him to move closer.

'Just for a few minutes, James. She thinks you look like Grandpa.'

'Mu-um...'

She'd ignore the rest of us then and talk softly to James about the farm and someone called Harry. James couldn't understand, so he'd sit there looking embarrassed, and Susie would sigh behind her book and roll her eyes.

Mum's temper had always scared me and she was so remote. She carried her rages around like a suppurative sore. I can understand her a bit better now that I'm older; life gets on top sometimes and I've had my share of the shit with James.

After she'd been in The Warren for a few months her mind seemed to snap. Snap, just as simple as that. She retreated into a world of her own and when she died it was as though she'd just segued into another time and space.

We buried Mum next to Dad in the tiny cemetery in Clement. It's close to the river, and around the edges are beautiful craggy grey gums. We wept for the same reasons most people weep at funerals, for the holes that are left in our own lives, and we can't think of anything else to do. The crows made their lonely noises.

Sometimes I feel I might be turning into my mother.

* * *

My hospital trolley is skidding along and I see the ceiling spinning above me. Dr Poulos is sliding beside me and speaking softly. His thick dark hair sticks out from under the theatre cap he's wearing and this gives him a faintly comical appearance. But I don't feel like laughing.

'Well, Helen, the last lot of tests were normal,' he'd said the last time I'd seen him. 'But I think we should do another biopsy just in case. Have to be sure.'

I wanted to ask why, but didn't have the energy and I didn't really want to know.

I like the look of this Dr Poulos. He's tall and dark, with a faraway look from behind his glasses and a kind voice, just the shot for someone who might have to give you bad news.

My mind wanders to the Greek family in the milk bar in Clement, just opposite Townie Beach. How could I have forgotten the name of that family? This doctor could be their youngest son, the one who'd peer out at the customers from behind the counter when I'd go there with Patrick and the others for milkshakes and fish and chips after we'd been swimming. Over thirty years ago, it could well be Mick junior. He studied something in Melbourne I'd heard.

I try hard to listen but the sun's shining into the room and the anxieties of the last few weeks have made me feel tired and distracted. Perhaps my body is letting me down like Mum's mind let her down. Who'll look after everyone if I die?

The hot sun outside reminds me of the time I thought we'd all had it on the day of the bushfires. One of those scorching, dry days with a wind that'd bowl you over. I made sure the kids were in the house, and sat them in the bathroom to play with a bucket of water to keep them cool. The red smoke covering the sun gave the air a surreal look, and I was terrified, especially for Rob who'd gone somewhere on a fire truck. We didn't die that day, but I left the photos and other precious belongings in the boxes, ready to go if we had to. Just like at the beginning of this marathon of tests and x-rays when I made sure all my things were in order — you never know when the threat to your mortality will be the real one.

Dr Poulos's voice goes on and I hear words that I don't want to be hearing.

'Simple procedure... endoscope... only about half an hour... couple of days off work... '

I hear other doctors explaining Mum's dementia.

'May's in a world of her own now, Helen.' Whatever that means.

They stop the trolley under the garish lights on the ceiling of the procedure room. Wish I had make-up on to cover my ageing skin. The walls are an icy white. The last time I was in a room like this was when James was born. No, James, I don't want to think about your problems now.

Dr Poulos is standing behind me and he puts his hand on my shoulder.

'Helen, this is Dr Lee. She's going to give you Hypnoval to make you relax.'

When I look towards Dr Lee, I see a face about the same age as Susie's. Don't tell me they're employing kids here these days.

'Just roll onto your left side please, Mrs Martin. I'm going to find a vein. This'll make you relax. You won't remember anything later.'

'I'll remember something.'

I'm not going to end up like my mother. I'm not going to forget things.

'You probably won't even remember this conversation.'

I float off into the shiny white wall and I think I'm going to dream about snow.

Hypnoval... hypnotic... relaxed... remember...

I must have dreamt about snow because I'm shivering and I don't stop until someone wraps a warm blanket around me.

'You can wake up now, Helen.'

It's Dr Poulos.

I want to wake up but it takes ages. This sleep has been too good. No wonder James uses stuff. No wonder Mum was happier in her dementia.

More of Dr Poulos's words float around me.

'Biopsy... pathology... but everything looks okay.'

Thinking's too hard so Rob talks to the doctor and I don't even hear much of what they're saying.

When Rob and I get home it's dark. Susie has made sandwiches and I can smell coffee. There are flowers on the kitchen table. Just like Susie to think about that.

Well done, I tell myself. I've survived to go another round, but isn't life fragile?

The very last time I saw my mother was when I thought I was going to turn into her. But I haven't yet.

Borrower

Lauren Arcamone

She says she is a moon
just borrowing the light
of stars, of suns — at noon
a white shadow; soon
a midnight looking glass.
Reflector of sun-sight,

hers is an ill-lit guise.
I am, I imagine,
the astronomer, eyes
fixed fast to the grand rise
and fall of galaxies,
charting the collision

of gods. In her I mark
the endless turning shift
from face to face, the stark
craters and pale pockmarks
of faded injury,
cool fingers drawn to lift

the grey tides. Together
we wander through memory —

what is, what was, what ever
waits still — and stand, tethered
to a moment that will
pass, savouring every

breath of light. Orbit-bound
in Time, we wait, blessed by
the dusk. The insects sound
their night-calls, the damp ground
cools our palms, and we watch
the sun sink from the sky.

Unveiled, I see her keep
watch, a soul's glow drawn high
while all the town's asleep.
Moon-shrouded, she is deep-
cast in light; she is the
brightest being in the sky.

Dead Bird

Alicia Gilmore

Arthur Johnson is a man of order. He sees smooth, benign strips before him. Stripes. It had been worth the wheezy shuffle down to the worn bench. The pain in his chest would perfunctorily subside, and then the slow, faltering steps back to the fibro cottage. The flicker of shadow and the fall of the sun-faded curtain would reveal Ellie, moth-like, fluttering uselessly indoors. From the front window the world is vertical. Tree, fence, lampposts, bus stop. Lines. Order. Direction.

Here, life is horizontal. Green, the new growth of weedy grasses amongst cigarette butts; a strip of ochre-warm hues meeting varying shades of turquoise and blue, sapphire smooth. So glassy, so glossy. Deceptive simplicity. Inviting. Lighter towards the shore than those obtuse patches of darkening turquoise, warning of depths unknown and untested. At length the sky, a vivid blue, lighter, slightly blemished by bleached wisps of clouds, marring the backdrop.

There is something atop those undulating waves. Arthur squints, his eyesight a pale imitation of those halcyon days when he could take aim and squeeze the trigger in a flawless, faultless, thoughtless move. No. Enough of the past. Arthur has never been a man for reminiscences. He strains worn eyes. It must be fishermen anchored offshore enjoying the lull and the lap of the hypnotic tide.

A muted roar, a dulled crest as wave connects with sandy beach.

This is not the storm-fuelled wickedness of previous tides. This is a calm deceptive lullaby, drawing a man in to entrap him in those treacherous darker depths. The midnight blue where nightmares reign.

In dreams they return to him, mother and child. Two satyrs. Hooves bloodied and worn, dirt swirling in agitated bursts. Banshee wails piercing a whipped sky. Was their anger directed solely at him? Were these metamorphoses to bestial states testimony to their true natures, or had violence brought out this anguish? In dreams and the cool expanse of the cheap cotton sheets he has slept in alone for years. Each night, trembling and sweat-soaked.

That first night he'd slept alone, having left his grief-struck wife and torn daughter at the hospital, he'd felt a twinge of shame at the secret stirring of delight he felt in having the entire bed to himself. Whiskey dealt with his shock. He dismissed the thought that Dolores had been right for once in her miserable existence; that he was an insensitive, unfeeling bastard.

He'd heard the commotion erupting from the back of the house, just as he was lighting his hand-rolled cigarette. Hysterical screams from the kitchen brought him to his feet. He couldn't stand fussing. Then he heard the dogs, baying in orgiastic cacophony, game bailed up in the tidal swamp.

'Oh God Arthur, stop them, stop them, save her!' His wife screaming incomprehensibly, then the sight he tried to forget for the remainder of his life. His dogs, his pride and joy, his trained hunting dogs clambering and tearing at a broken and bloodied doll on the ground. His beloved little daughter. He'd wanted a son but something in her delicate manner and beaming smile had captured his heart. The unsteady gait, the giggles of joy; Daddy, Daddy.

Dolores screaming, forever screaming. 'Shut up woman, for God's sake, shut up.' He stepped into the fray.

'Drop her, damn you.' He reached for the hose. A blast of cold water would call off the hysterical hounds.

'Dead bird. DEAD BIRD.' The game shooters command for ducks and pheasants. It worked. Her immobile form dropped to the ground, her precious face mauled and ripped open. An ear, torn and macabre, hanging down onto a once rosy cheek. Waxy. The dogs slunk away fearing wrath. One yelped as he kicked it with polished leather boots, cradling his daughter's inert body. His precious little girl.

'Daddy... '

'Drop. Drop her.' Spencer was shaking her limp body to and fro between clenched jaws. He'd put the bullet to Spencer himself. The last time he'd fired a shot.

***

Lingering traces of tucked-away cafes and clubs, laughing nights warmed by candlelight, conversation and unspoken promises, of music in the night and strolls through unevenly paved streets. A small glass bottle, stoppered tight. Delicate enough to be carried in a clutch or small handbag, a daily necessity for a sophisticated young woman. Strong enough to survive.

Ellie lifts the small bottle and inhales the memory of her mother. The perfume speaks of youthful delight and possibility, of a beautiful girl, *belle fille*, whose spirit never aged. Flitting between cafes and admirers, would her eyes now sparkle behind the worn folds of time? Would this scent cause an old man to pause mid-step, time halted, memory reborn, of those days and those nights when he thought love and youth lasted forever?

These are Ellie's imaginings of her mother. The mother who left. Ellie has vague remembrances of soft hands holding her, stroking her forehead over thick white bandages. Watery brown eyes looking down into hers. I love you, I love you, I'm sorry.

Ellie couldn't remember 'Goodbye'. She imagines it was spoken though all she knows for certain is that when she was finally released from the hospital, her mother and the dogs had all gone. Lingering traces were rounded up and disposed off ruthlessly. Cans of dog food, her mother's clothes. Except for this forgotten perfume bottle that Ellie pocketed and squirreled into her own room. Proof that there was once a woman who must have had dreams, who must have felt love.

***

Blasted child. Going to feed the dogs her biscuits as if they were pampered pets, not hunting dogs. Working dogs. Damned child.

Arthur was horrified when he saw her limp, bloodied body, yet was silently in awe of the power of those magnificent beasts. Their wild natures springing forth. Furious too when they didn't obey his orders immediately. Perhaps they were not as well trained as he'd believed. Blame the bitch. He'd thought their pedigree was secure but you never can tell. Blame the bitch.

He'd slapped Dolores after this. 'Stop the hysterics,' he'd started to say but it wasn't the truth. What kind of mother was she to let her child out to be mauled by the dogs? Blame the bitch. He'd slapped her, hit her, again and again. She'd stayed at the hospital after that, and then he'd made it clear she wasn't welcome back in his house. A bad mother wasn't to be trusted around a child. That was obvious to him now. He'd thrown her and her meagre belongings out. He'd closed the door to her, to the world. Only inside, under his protection, would Ellie be safe.

He'd threatened to sue that fool Frederick who'd sold him the dogs. 'Sired by Kingsley' indeed. Frederick had eventually coughed up to pay some of the medical bills, though Dolores had begged him to keep it out of court. He'd wanted new dogs but for Ellie and for appearances sake, he'd given up the dogs and the hunting. Had lost the taste for it really. Shooting game when all he could see was images of his little girl's scalp and raw cheek.

***

Ellie placed the perfume bottle back inside the old biscuit tin. Her precious few treasures, kept safe, hidden beneath a musty hand knitted scarf in her wardrobe. It was only when her father had left the house — infrequent, unpredictable now he'd retired — that she dared bring her prized possessions out into the light of day. A blurred, black and white photo of herself as a child standing with her mother. Taken at the beach before the attack, before her mother walked out of her life forever, when Ellie and her mother shared smiling, unscarred faces. Ellie remembered scents and sensations of that day. A downpour. Threading through the melaleuca trees on sunburnt legs. Her mother's voice, 'Sometimes you see a person in the water and all you can do is to watch them drown.' Ellie hadn't thought of those words for years. Had her mother been drowning, is that why she left? Or could she not watch Ellie flounder and sink?

Ellie knew that people had difficulty looking at her. Ellie couldn't bear her own reflection in a mirror, this scarred parody of twisted flesh. Her father had made it perfectly clear throughout her insular life that he did not wish to look at her deformed face, that he was keeping her in to protect the world from the horror of her patchwork features. No one would ever want her or want to look at her unless to mock and jeer. He'd made her promise to keep away from the windows, lest anyone spy the monstrous mask, but that was an impossible vow to keep. He'd beaten her when she was a teenager, when he discovered her in the front room, exposing her breasts to a gaggle of school boys who'd dared to venture off the footpath.

There is an old globe in the corner of the room, gathering dust upon the fingerprint-smeared surface. A lead trailing along the pedestal to the worn floorboards below is slightly frayed; Ellie fingers it nostalgically. If she plugged it in would it glow, illuminating the U.S.S.R. in soft crimson hues? A time before the Cold War publicly ceased, a time when her father had brought the globe to add pretension to this humble house. Did he dream, just as she does, of adventures far beyond suburbia? Dreams far from these dreary walls, this worn flooring and these threadbare rugs.

Ellie has fantasised about leaving so many times, her hand hovering nervously above the deadbolt. It would take so little, just a turn of the wrist to unlock the door, to move into the world. So much. Too much. She'd never been strong enough to leave, to speak up. The only thing she'd ever been brave enough to stand up to her father about was Percival. Her moggy cat, one of a litter she'd heard mewling under the house years ago. Whilst her father was at work, she'd risked being seen by the neighbours and ventured into the then forbidden backyard. Under the house was the scraggiest litter of kittens she'd ever seen. Five mewling bundles, eyes clenched tight against the world. Ellie had waited all day for the mother cat to return. She never did. Ellie fashioned a sling from the scarf she'd been patiently knitting, and carried the delicate creatures inside. Her father had drowned all of the kittens but one when he found out she'd been outside. The lone kitten, Percival, had survived due to his innate curiosity. He'd been off exploring her wardrobe when the others were captured. Ellie sobbed as she watched her father kill the others, bitterly refusing to hand over Percival. If she went outside again...

***

Arthur paused as he made his way back home. From here, from the footpath, he could just see a shadow, a twitching of the old lace curtains. The shadow uncurled and took on a feline shape. Blasted cat. Should've drowned the lot of them. He made his way into the house via the side path into the kitchen. He could hear Ellie fumbling at the piano and could see some scraggly flowers in a vase on the table. So, she'd been outside again, into the backyard. He'd stopped hitting. Truth be told he didn't have the energy anymore. In the past few decades he'd let the trees and shrubs tower over the paling fence. No one would be looking in at her. The McAndrews had moved out in the eighties; he doubted the new neighbours even knew he had a daughter. He walked into his room to switch his walking shoes for his slippers and trod on a sticky, congealing mess.

'Blasted cat!'

Ellie ignored her father though his stale tobacco scent permeated the air and she knew he'd done more than just pause in the doorway, knew that he'd entered the room.

'Damned cat's been sick in my room again.'

Ellie nodded.

'Ellie d'you hear me? Clean up after that scrawny beast you hear.'

'Yes, Father.' Ellie's voice had long ago lost any traces of life, of personality or of heart. There was no arguing with her father. In Arthur Johnson's house, his word was law. He glared at the mongrel mixed breed looking smugly back at him from atop the piano, and could have sworn there was mocking in those yellow feline eyes.

'You haven't been too close to the front window have you, Ellie?' He eyed the old lace with suspicion.

'No, Father.'

He grunted. 'And no one saw you when you went out the back, did they?'

'No, Father.'

Now his steely gaze settled on the back of her head. Pre-Raphaelite hair loosely captured at the nape of her neck, but the small plastic band couldn't contain all of the warm-hued coppery strands descending in rippled waves over her brown-flecked top. Head lowered, Ophelia succumbing in final resignation. From her good side, in profile, her features are strong and straight, as if a sculptor has breathed life into marble. 'Good,' he muttered. 'No one would want to see you anyhow.' Her head sunk a little more towards her chest.

Arthur remembered going to Sunday school lessons as a small child, learning about the books of Genesis, of the Apostles, of the Revelation, the book of Job. All of the trials and suffering that God and Satan had put Job through, well, Arthur was sure if Job had had a daughter, she'd look like Ellie. Mangled and mangy like her flea-ridden cat. Arthur remembered there'd been a neighbouring boy in his Sunday school class, Jack, a shambling, scruffy boy with quick eyes and quicker hands. Jack's mother was the Sunday school teacher, a tall, overbearing woman with wiry hair that seemed to have been grey her entire life. He could imagine that same stern, strict imposing figure scrunched into the form of a child. Jack and Arthur had taken it in turns to steal from the collection plate, even as his insides veered between the wrath of God, the minister or the evil eye of Jack's mother. Arthur and Jack were never caught, and ate ice-cream every Sunday after church. He smiled at the memory. Jack.

'Sorry, Father?' He startled at Ellie's voice.

'What, child?' he looked down and winced. She was looking straight at him, that grotesque face disgusted him still.

'Did you say something?' she asked again, the timidity in her tone pleased and annoyed him. He straightened abruptly.

'Keep away from that window, my girl, and clean up after that damned cat.'

***

These weren't the wings she'd imagined. Fragile, delicate, transparent. Too easily damaged, carelessly, thoughtlessly. Ellie returns to the overgrown backyard in the afternoon, after clearing away the lunch things and once her father lies down for his rest. He seemed to fatigue easily these days, the slightest effort causing a wheeze and cough deep in his chest. He had cut back now his trembling hands couldn't roll his own cigarettes very well. His fingers were still stained though. Maybe some stains never faded. Ellie watches an orange and black wanderer butterfly alight on one plant then another, wishing she could travel to an exotic land, with flowers and light, new scents to savour and explore. She imagines herself anew, a world away from this hidden yard and the rasping cough of the elderly man inside. She thinks she hears him call her name but remains seated, Percival purring on her lap. She strokes his head absent-mindedly and imagines another face, another life.

***

Arthur raises his head and sips from the glass of water on his bedside table. The familiar squeeze, the tightening, clenching fist around the chest. The windpipe, those shrinking tubes that painfully serve as a reminder that cells don't last forever, bodies don't last forever, lungs don't last. The audible rasp is excruciatingly felt. Smooth pipes he imagines carillon smooth, instead of these scarred, worn, damaged airways that are grated with each straining exhalation. The barking cough, rib cracking force and still the air refuses to simply leave. Struggling to breathe, unable to fight the congestion sinking heavy in his lungs, the coarse rattle. He knows now how it will feel when he goes, the blessed relief to give up the fight. Would he have done things differently? He should have drowned all the cats. He could have tried again with Dolores and had another child, a son. A perfect boy, scar free. He wouldn't have been ashamed of a son. He wouldn't have kept those blasted dogs. He would have drowned those blasted dogs, those cats, Ellie...

***

Fern fronds in hand, Ellie looks at her pathetic floral display in disgust. It is time for her father's afternoon cup of tea. Same time, every day. Weak tea, two sugars, stirred three times, one biscuit.

'Father, would you like your tea in your room?' No answer. Percival darts between her legs and strolls into her father's bedroom, tail haughtily aloft.

'Percival, back here,' she hisses, not wishing to clean up another of his misguided and ill-timed fur balls. Percival has leapt onto her father's bed, where her father lies, mannequin-still, stony-eyed.

Ellie freezes in a moment of clarity, of communion. She is struck by the shafts of afternoon light breaking through the Venetian struts. Meridian lines, dividing the room, this life, into the negative spaces and the light. Dark pauses and positive space. Half-life. Half-light. Ellie can hear the ticking of a clock. The contours of a life measured in tiny artificial heartbeats. An artificial life.

Arthur Johnson is lying on his faded chenille bedspread, hands clasped at chest height, clutching the small clock. The ticking hands where his heart should be. The maidenhair fronds slip unnoticed from Ellie's hand. Maidenhair gossamer dreams, delicate and easily bruised. Spidery veins punctuate the surface of the leaves, of his hands. Was there a time when they'd loved each other? When they were happy? A family? Pauses between the metallic clicks throb with suspended silence, pauses that could last forever. An eternity of cessation.

It is soothing, this artificial heart pumping its rhythm. Long forgotten chimes from the womb. Ellie hears the kettle boiling in the kitchen and pictures the steam rising, fogging the window. Percival sniffs at Arthur's stiffening form, and with metrical paws kneads a place on the worn chenille. He purrs, rhythmically, loudly.

Product(s) of the Past

Tara N. McKenzie

I send the old bits
to an attic room
where they dance
like children
in dust-covered coats,
peering from shadows
and pleading for attention
when they've gone
too long unnoticed.

They are
friends remembered,
secrets shared,
lips kissed and
hands outstretched,
stories told,
tickets, queues,
moments
forever sacred.

They are artifacts
invaluable,
yet the farcical busyness

of my day-to-day
covers them in minutiae
until they are smothered
to submission.
They cower in the corners
of my mind
...
and wait.

When night falls
a curtain of black,
I call for my attic children.
I gather them 'round me
and watch
in quiet amazement
as they dance the story
of me.

Acknowledgements

The Editors would like to thank the Department of Media and Communications and the School of Letters, Art and Media at the University of Sydney for the publication of this anthology.

Particular thanks are due to Keith Stevenson for his invaluable assistance with the project.

The Editors:
Sanzeeda Ali, Kacie Bluhm, Cyrus Carandang, Travis Clark, Megan Cuthbert, Renata Ficek, Chrysoula Georgopoulos, Deborah Green, Sarah Jessup, Isabella Lesslie, Katja Lieb, Anabella Marquis, Agata Mrva-Montoya, Larissa Norrie, Katie Pittard, Ilya Popov, Marcus Olsson, Sarah Rhodes, Jess Scurry, Ying Ying Shi, Soharni Tennekoon, Lauren Williams.